Doctor Yellow Jack

A Novel

by

Ronald Vlietstra

Doctor Yellow Jack

I dedicate this book to Nick and Lucy and hope they experience as many rich life adventures as their parents.

1 *London, 1878*

Wally McConnochie awoke spread-eagled on the muddy shore of the River Thames. The briny, morning tide seeped through his britches and trickled in his boots. A family of rats foraged through discarded slops upon some steps above him and their claws scratched and scraped as they carried away treasures of gristle and bone.

"*Kiore, paru, paru!*" he muttered, as he struggled to a sitting position. Dirty, dirty creatures: words his mother used whenever she spotted a rat. If she could see him now he knew what she would say. Maori boys should keep to their own and not sail off to foreign lands, beyond their tribal roots, their *iwi*. She also wouldn't want him wasting precious money on poker games in seedy bars.

"Hey you! What's that yer blabbing?"

Wally turned his head and looked up.

A big constable, his shoulders squared and his feet set firm astride the top of the steps, peered down at him. "What yer up to?" he continued, pointing his truncheon at Wally. Framed by the grey morning mist, the bobby's tall black hat and heavy boots made him look like a giant.

"Nothing, sir. Just taking a rest, if you don't mind."

"You hurt? Is that blood on your chest?"

"No, it's a tattoo, sir. It's fine." He pulled his shirt front closed.

"Then be off about your business, young man."

"I will—in a twinkle, sir." No sense in arguing with a copper this time of day.

Wally's last clear memory was of jostling with a gang of Arabs outside the Three Compasses pub, with them pushing and punching to get at his winnings. He reached for his pants pockets but they'd been turned inside out; his purse was gone.

With a soggy sleeve he wiped a blob of slime off his dusky brown face. His head throbbed and his body ached as if a bullock wagon had driven over him. The bells of St Paul's Cathedral chimed six times. This was Victorian London, refuge of the dispossessed, not his native New Zealand, and he had hit a new low.

He wriggled up onto the lowermost steps, scattering rats and crabs as he did so. He sat and assessed the damage. The back of his head was very sore, his left eye wouldn't open fully and his arms and legs were stiff, no doubt from the tumble he took as his assailants threw him over the escarpment. Nothing, however, felt broken.

Wally was no stranger to bare-knuckle fights, or to losing them, but for him the loss of the two guineas in his pocket hurt more. He couldn't afford to lose that money, not when he had another payment to make to the loan shark who was bleeding him for every penny, the Earl of Kemble.

In London's riverside pubs, Wally lived the life of a gambler. He was good at counting cards and his dark features and vivid chest tattoo distracted, even disturbed, his opponents. He called himself King Tawhai and he sang fragments of Maori proverbs as magical incantations that suggested a special relationship with the supernatural.

Ma te huruhuru, ka rere te manu. Nobody listening knew the simple meaning of these words: with feathers a bird can fly.

A battered King Tawhai stood up and pulled his pea coat around him for the long walk back to Widow Murphy's lodging-house. He didn't feel very kingly, nor did he look it. His soggy pants and coat were caked with mud and his shirt was torn at the collar. I might as well be back in the bleak New Zealand goldfields as shambling along the cobbled streets of London, he thought. True, nobody here minds that I'm part Maori. All they know is I'm on the edge, just as hungry and desperate as they are, scratching around for any scrap of money or bit of luck.

Snooty toffs might call him a big brown beetle, a horrible expression, but a fair summary of how lowly dark-skinned people were considered during Queen Victoria's reign. He was better off than the beggars and the nail-gropers who scavenged for metal scraps, but he was on a par with the patterers, pickpockets and street-performers, never confident as to where next week's rent money would come from or how much food they could afford. What those fellow scroungers didn't know was that Wally's ambition was for a life of professional success as a doctor of medicine. With two years of training already completed in New Zealand, he was tantalizingly close, but the last few doors seemed the hardest to open, what with next to no money for university and Kemble snapping at his heels.

He entered the boarding-house through the back door, the one that led into the narrow scullery where the smell of cabbage lingered and the enamel sink was always cluttered with dishes and pans.

"Don't *you* look a right mess?" said Widow Murphy twisting her head around to look up at Wally. "What av you been up ta?"

"Oh, I fell down the embankment steps. It was dark and foggy"

"Pooh! And you stinks to high heaven." She pinched her nose and turned her attention back to her running taps.

They had a bond built on shared experience of tuberculosis. Her problem was that she was crippled as a child, by spinal tuberculosis, and lived life permanently stooped like the beggars Wally had seen in Goa and Egypt. Wally treated her with respect, as if her deformity was a badge of distinction.

In New Zealand, Wally had worked with an English doctor by the name of Chisholm. They both enjoyed nature: birds, plants, the great Clutha River and the majesty of the mountains. Wally's dark thick lips and his red and blue chest tattoo were matters of curiosity for the old physician, not an excuse for the mockery that many white New Zealanders heaped on him. The doctor lived with tuberculosis, both around him and within himself, yet every day he found new reasons to love life, to read and to smile. After Chisholm died, his precious collection of gold funded Wally for two years at medical school.

"Nothing for me to salt away today then?" she asked.

"No. Actually I need a quid—I really need two." Widow Murphy kept Wally's savings hidden away for him, safe from the thievery of other lodgers. She kept her bedroom locked at night and she rarely left the house during the day, save perhaps to go to the market in Rotherhithe village or to spend a shilling to hear a recital at the Royal Aquarium.

3

"Well, least let me mend your shirt." Her bony fingers plucked at the torn collar. "It's your good one, isn't it?"

"Later—there's no need." He paused. "I'll leave it out."

Widow Murphy reminded him a lot of his mother. She noticed everything and she fussed. Both women talked too much and Wally often acted deaf.

Widow Murphy and his mother were about the same age but in other ways they couldn't have been more different. Wally's mother, Kirimoko, was full-blooded Maori, tall and dark, and she rarely spoke in English. Wally sometimes wondered what Widow Murphy would make of his mother's cheek and chin tattoos. Yet in a way he could see the two of them relating well to each other, each accepting the other's proud disfigurements.

" Av I not told you to take off your filthy boots?" she called to him as he slowly climbed the stairs to his room. He pretended not to hear.

Wally sat on the edge of his bed. He removed his boots and wet socks and lay them on the window ledge to dry. He reached into the porcelain basin on his bedside table and splashed some water on his face. He didn't feel like washing nor did he feel like shaving, but he pushed himself to do both. He still had to face the Earl.

His rented upstairs room in Rotherhithe was small, scarcely bigger than a cabin on a ship. Most of the room was filled by two beds, his and the one currently occupied by his roommate, David Williams, a young Welshman who worked as a stall cleaner at the London Zoo. Williams shared the strong territorial instincts of the carnivores he worked with and growled at Wally if his space was threatened. So fierce was his reaction when provoked, and so violent the resulting outbursts, that Wally tried to minimize his time in the room and, whenever possible, he let the sleeping Williams lie undisturbed. When he was younger, he would have relished punching out the Welshman, but Wally told himself that he was an adult now and resorting to fists was a last resort.

In avoiding the boundary between the two beds there was little space left for his clothes, boots and books. In that way he supposed he was lucky to have so few possessions.

The room itself was rundown and forlorn. Perhaps the wall-paper had once been pretty with its pattern of roses and trellises but

4

now it was cracked and peeling, with scrim showing through in places making a shadowy web that danced in the flickering gaslight at night. A large window faced out onto a hedge-ringed park where dogs and children played by day and drunks and hobos argued at night while Wally was kept awake by the sound of Williams' snoring.

The soap slid in his hands as he smeared it over his grubby face. The cold water prevented any lather from forming and his stubble felt prickly and rough. He pressed the cutthroat blade along his cheeks and chin and gritted his teeth as its dull edge tugged and tore at his whiskers. The nicks and scratches stung when he splashed his face with more of the chilly water but he looked more presentable for the effort, his puffed-up eye the only relic of the last night's beating.

The previous week, playing cards against a down-and-out old Cockney, Wally won a silver and enamel lady's fob watch. On its face, red Turkish numerals bordered a miniature painting of a Swiss chalet and its hands were a spiral filigree of gold. The hinged protective hunter case was painted with a spray of roses on the front and an inviting rural lake and mountain scene on the back. Delicate patterns of ribbing and swirls adorned the trim. The Arab robbers hadn't found it inside his pea coat. It was nearly eight o'clock.

Quietly, so as not to disturb Williams, he switched out of his dirty pants and torn shirt and put on his other set of clothes: the canvas pants he'd worn on the ship coming over from New Zealand and a black woolen sweater over a ragged undershirt. He cradled his mud-stained clothes under his arm and limped downstairs to the breakfast room. None of the other lodgers were down for their breakfast yet and the morning's newspaper sat unopened on the table. He scanned the front page. A fifty-five foot long squid had been towed ashore at Thimble Tickle, Newfoundland. The eyes of the monster were eighteen inches across and its suckers an amazing four inches in diameter.

"Porridge?" Widow Murphy interrupted.

"If it's not lumpy," said Wally. His two sovereigns lay on the lace tablecloth along with a shilling and a sixpence.

"What's the extra money for?" he said.

"Can you bring me back a leg of mutton and a dozen sausages?"

Wally would be walking almost to Newgate Market on his way to see the Earl of Kemble. To walk a little further to the market and look over all the produce would be pleasant, observing market gardeners and butchers tending their scales and light-fingered urchins filling their pockets with goodies.

The Widow knew his routine. For ten weeks now he'd made his Wednesday visit to the City taking the ferry across the Thames and walking on to Kemble's office on Ludgate Hill.

"Is that all you want?" he said.

"Just the change," she answered. Yes, she was very much like Kirimoko.

She also treated him with respect. He liked that. People of color were often not well treated in London. Africans, Asians, Arabs and Indians might throng the streets of the Empire's capital but their status was no higher than the gutter.

Children often singled Wally out for special jeers if they spotted the spiral tattoo on his chest. His *moko*, a sign of pride for any Maori, stigmatized him here as a savage and he did his best to hide it.

Wally would need at least twenty pounds to pay his fees for medical school. Even if he could get a job as a barrow boy or a barge hand, it would take more than a year to save that much. That's why the gambling plan had seemed so good.

It was a pity it had backfired. Kemble gave the appearance of being an honest patron at first but he soon revealed himself to be a leech. He wasn't even an Earl; Wally had been suckered.

Wally's first meeting with Kemble, three months prior, had seemed straightforward enough, even though a cathedral was an odd place to discuss a loan. Yet that's where the gentleman suggested they meet. A fellow cardsharp arranged it all and he said the Earl liked his secrecy—a red flag that Wally missed.

St Paul's was only a short walk from the Rotherhithe ferry and Wally arrived early. He sat in a pew near the chapel of St Francis and used the time to practice shuffling his De La Rue playing cards, the deck making a crisp snapping sound as he sprung it back with his thumb. A good poker player has to shuffle well. He can't bluff his way through that part.

From where he sat he had a good view of the entryway. Not that one had to look. In the empty apse, every footstep echoed off the marble floors and he could have heard a church mouse tiptoeing behind the altar. Not like the mud floor in the old *whare* back in Otakau where a little boy could creep right up behind someone and scare the wits out of them.

His mother used to say, *"He namu pea ahau."* It meant: You are like a sand fly. Even though you are small, you can be very annoying.

Then Wally saw him. There was no mistaking that it was the Earl of Kemble—tall, head held erect, shoulders braced back, Kemble carried gloves and a top hat and he wore a black frock coat. He had on a bow tie and a walking cane hung over his left arm.

"Morning, young man," he said, as he sat down in the pew behind Wally. Kemble's posh accent and the spicy fragrance of his aftershave reminded Wally that it was more than just a pew that separated them.

Wally nodded.

"I understand we might be able to help each other," said Kemble.

"Maybe—well, I dunno."

"You don't look like a wastrel," said Kemble. "And you could use a few bob, I'm sure."

"Yes, who couldn't?" Wally countered.

"Well, let me get to the point, then. Some men invest in racehorses, but most of their money goes to the bookies. I like to go one step better. I back winners and keep the bookies out of it."

"But how do you know they are winners?"

The Earl leaned back and laughed out loud.

"That's the easy part, young man."

"Easy?"

"I teach them how to win."

"You teach horses how to win?"

"No, stupid! I teach poker players. Youngsters! Clever young-sters like yourself."

"And they pay you to teach them poker? No, I don't need that, thank you. And I couldn't afford it anyway."

The Earl leaned back against the pew. He squinted his eyes as if to show earnestness.

"Ah, but my plan is different. I pay you the money."

The Earl flicked invisible specks off his sleeve.

"You pay *me* money."

"Yes, to get you started. Call it a kitty, if you like."

"And I pay you back later on?"

"Sure, plus a little bit of your winnings."

"How much?"

"Let's say fifty percent."

2 Kemble's Office

Wally knocked on Kemble's office door.

"Good morning, sir," said Wally.

The muffled voice of his nemesis called him in.

Mudlip looked like an earl. Drooping eyelids and sagging cheeks gave him the gravitas of a man of authority, the look of a military commander. His thin, gray hair, what remained of it, lay plastered flat across his head and a trim moustache covered his upper lip.

The Earl sat at a desk covered with bills, dockets and receipts. His thick hands pushed the scraps of paper about as if the desktop were a battlefield map of his Kingdom of Money and the pile of coins and banknotes at his elbow the troops he was holding in reserve. His real name was Lucas Mudlip but he called himself the Earl of Kemble.

"Mornin',

His uniform consisted of a black suit and red waistcoat—he pronounced it weskit—and a turned-down shirt collar starched stiff. Heralds and insignia signaled his having attended Britain's best colleges and belonging to the cream of social establishments. One day he'd wear a King's College tie, the next a cravat from Balliol. Just when he had you believing he was a Navy man, he'd strut around as a Queen's Fusilier. To top it off he had a wide array of gold and silver pins, medals and badges, attesting to heroism in the Crimea, membership of the Royal Society and adventures in the Arctic. These impressive symbols, however, were all phony facades to fool the innocent. Kemble, or Mudlip, had earned none of these accolades.

Wally stared at the picture on the wall behind the desk—a pastoral scene, perhaps the sort of thing one would see in Gloucestershire, around Kemble. Plump cows munched thick grass in a pasture where poppies and thistles grew. Neat wire fences and a row of ash trees bordered the field, and rounded hills and a sunny sky framed the background.

Lucas Mudlip was, however, no country squire. He was the son of a poor blacksmith and had never sailed beyond Greenwich. Where he got all his paraphernalia was anybody's guess and, like most things about him, the Earl was not about to tell.

Mudlip's deception and dandiness intrigued Wally but it was his readiness to loan out money that had hooked Wally three months ago.

"You haven't let me down, have you?" He eyed Wally up and down as if he were a disobedient servant.

Watching Mudlip had encouraged Wally to call himself King Tawhai. Half the mugs he gambled against would believe him and the rest would simply think him a fool. Both ways he'd come out ahead.

"No. I got it," said Wally.

"What happ'nd yer eye?" asked the Earl.

"A bunch of Arabs had a go at me," said Wally.

"Not my boys, then. Don't trust them wogs."

Kemble had a stable of thugs that he called on to enforce his threats whenever a debtor fell behind in paying off a loan. They'd use iron bars and wooden bats to batter and bruise anyone a day or two overdue on their payments and they might smash a leg or split the skull of a more serious debtor, someone behind as much as a fortnight. No one knew of a living soul who'd escaped without paying his dues to Kemble, but many were aware of the horrible punishments meted out to those who hadn't. Those unfortunates would be found under a pile of garbage in a back lane in Millwall or they'd be washed up by the tide at the Isle of Dogs.

Wally handed over two pounds, his weekly repayment. Kemble snatched the money and he crossed off a line on a scrap of paper.

"Half way there," he said.

"I've repaid all the money you loaned me," said Wally, his voice strained, hands on hips.

Kemble thumped the table causing some loose papers to fly onto the floor.

"Look, you brown bugger, don't start playing games with me. You'll pay the other half or I'll have yer guts for garters." Kemble's face flushed and his chest heaved. His eyes bulged and his jaw worked up and down as if he were chewing tobacco.

"Sorry, sir," said Wally, retreating from the desk as he spoke. He'd surprised himself with having said anything at all about the loan, and now he wished he hadn't. "See you next week," he added, his servile demeanor restored.

One other time he'd challenged Mudlip to follow through on his promise of teaching him how to win. Mudlip's response had been curt: You'll learn yourself soon enough—if you know how sorry you'll be if I don't get my money! And for emphasis, one of his henchmen belted Wally across his upper arm with a nightstick, the arm that had been broken five years before in a goldfield's brawl.

Outside Mudlip's office, Wally kicked a lamppost with frustration. He could pawn his elegant fob watch and, along with the ten pounds or so that Widow Murphy was holding for him, he might have just enough to pay Kemble all he wanted. But that would mean nothing left for himself, no money for medical school, and his efforts wasted. He had to find another way!

It was ten o'clock and the Newgate market was in full swing. It was unusual to see a lady or a gentleman there and that morning was no exception. The shopping for a household was done by a maid, the cook, the butler, or, in Wally's case, a lodger. The street was too muddy, the stalls too crowded, and the language too coarse for a person with sensibilities, not to mention the smells and the sights of glassy-eyed, gutted game, snotty beggars and fresh horse dung.

The atmosphere was, however, a tonic for Wally, like biting into a lemon. It woke him up, enlivened him, and made him take notice of the world around him. There was more to life than money and Mudlip.

At a butcher's stall he bought the mutton and sausages, bargaining the man down to a shilling. The remaining sixpence belonged to Widow Murphy but Wally judged that a penny or two of it was rightfully his for having done the shopping and the bargaining.

He spotted a barrow of used books and, rummaging through them, he found Ivanhoe, an old favorite of his father's. Threepence later the book was his. He was so happy he celebrated by filching and swallowing a pickled mussel from a fishmonger's stall.

Back at his lodgings, Wally sat on his bed and thumbed through the pages of Ivanhoe. Williams, his roommate, was away at the zoo, and the room was his own. The house was quiet.

He pictured his father sitting in the big high-backed chair in the kitchen of his New Zealand house, reading aloud from *Ivanhoe*—his Scottish brogue echoing the voice of Sir Walter Scott, the book's author. How much he'd wanted Wally to understand the part of him that was Scottish.

Wally's only living connection with Scotland now was Helen, a girl who had joined the Bristol, the ship he'd sailed on from New Zealand. She boarded in Egypt and had traveled along with them from Port Said to London. She was unmarried and pregnant, yet she'd been full of optimism and enthusiasm, an ideal companion for Wally when his long voyage from New Zealand risked wearing him threadbare. She'd made Wally want to explore the Scottish side of his character. He'd struggled so long with his more evident Maori-ness that a taste of how it was to be a Scot might fill the gaping hole within his heart.

He had her address but he'd procrastinated over writing to her. Now might be a good time.

Dearest Helen!

Was that too familiar? He really only knew her for two weeks and, even then, his relationship was mostly that of being her physician.

My dear friend Helen,
I trust this letter finds you in excellent health. I want to ask about your baby.

Of course he did, but it wasn't really any of his business. What's more, the baby mightn't be doing well—might even have died. A tactful person would know these things before venturing forth in such a bold way.

My dear friend Helen,
I trust all is well.
I am enjoying London.

That was quite untrue but, by now, Wally had become adept at telling lies in his letters. Failing to do well is one thing, but broadcasting that to your friends and relatives is another.

I am sure that I'll be coming to Scotland to start medical school in the very near future.

Another lie! He had too little money and no prospects.

Please write and tell me how you are doing.

He employed no assumptions, just a straightforward request. He scanned the words for signs of loneliness or desperation. He could see none.

Yours truly,

Walter

Perhaps he should have said *Wally*. Better to err on the safe side. Her situation was precarious and it would be wrong for her parents to read too much into his friendship. He couldn't afford any financial entanglements now and it would be a long time before he ever could.

3   The New Man

Next morning, at breakfast, a well-dressed young man sat in Wally's usual chair.

"Aye, good morning," said the stranger. His accent was Scottish.

"Morning," said Wally.

"Do we just sit anywhere?" the new man asked.

"You've met already," said Miss Murphy, carrying in a plate of porridge. Wally noticed that she was using the less-chipped crockery this morning, her good set. She must be out to impress the new guest.

The new man was large in build, like Wally, but everything about him looked even heavier. His head sat heavy on his shoulders and a large moustache dragged down the corners of his mouth, yet some deep inner source of energy reddened his cheeks and jutted forward his chin. He had the beefy hands and flattened nose of someone who is a boxer, a military man perhaps, maybe even a graduate of Sandhurst.

His voice told another story. He spoke so softly and precisely that a blind person might think him a teacher or a cleric. An educated man, that's for sure, and a Scot to boot.

"I don't care where I sit," said Wally, ladling porridge into a bowl.

"I'm new here," the heavy man said.

"Yes, I see that," said Wally. "I should introduce myself. My name's Wally—Wally McConnochie, and I'm from New Zealand."

"And a good Scottish name, too. I would not have suspected it," said the other.

Wally winced at the veiled reference to his brown skin and he pulled his shirt-front closed over his tattoo.

"Mister Doyle is from Scotland," Widow Murphy added. She wiped her hands on her clean apron and smoothed some of the wrinkles out of the fresh tablecloth.

"Arthur Doyle—Arthur Conan Doyle. It's an Irish name. My dad's Irish." The new man's cheeks reddened even more whether from emphasis or embarrassment it was hard for Wally to be sure.

"I won't hold that against you," said Wally, but if it was a joke, his face showed no laughter. Schoolboy brawls with taunting Irish bigots had left their scars, and the new man's pugilist demeanor risked reopening old wounds.

"Toast for either of you?" interjected Widow Murphy.

The rest of breakfast passed in silence interrupted only by the clatter of knife or spoon on plate and the knock of cup on saucer.

The London of the late 1870s was thrilling if you were rich, royal or in the limelight like the spectacular cricketer W.G. Grace but most of the city's nearly one million inhabitants had little money and few prospects. Wally was amongst the almost penniless but he did have one advantage. Before he sailed to England he studied in New Zealand's new medical school in Dunedin. His training, however, was cut short by political problems in the school's administration and he needed more study to merit being called a doctor. For that he needed money.

Today it was Monday, and like any other Monday in summer, skipping work was ever so more pleasant for the common laborer than sitting at a loom, sewing treadle or canning machine. Workers would instead head to the pubs and, by the time they'd drunk a few pints, they'd be ready to gamble, never mind the missus or the young ones at home. Wally's task was to clean out their pockets, just as his had been emptied by the Arabs outside the Three Compasses, but rather than use brute force he used his wits and King Tawhai magic.

Later that morning, walking along the Embankment near the Tunnel, Wally spotted the Scot he'd met at breakfast. The man was walking briskly and he had a magazine under his arm. There was no easy way to avoid him.

"Hello again," said Wally, struggling to think of something intelligent to say. Perhaps he could ask him about conditions in Ireland. From the way Widow Murphy treated him, he might be a man of means, a member of the landed gentry.

"Yees," said the other man, stretching the word out in a very Scottish way. The sound reassured Wally. It was familiar and warm, not Irish at all.

"What do you think—but you're mostly Scot, aren't you?" said Wally.

"And Scots don't think?"

"Quite the opposite. I know some who think a lot."

"But just some?" The Scot playfully prodded Wally with his rolled-up magazine, in imitation of a brave knight defending his country's honor.

"I'm reading *Ivanhoe* just now. You must know it."

"Of course. The Plantagenet kings might have reigned long ago but their bloody exploits still stain our countryside."

Wally smiled. There was something likeable about Doyle, a cheeky sense of humor, something he had missed during their awkward meeting at breakfast. The Scotsman's accent reminded him of Professor Coughtrey, back in Dunedin, but Doyle's dislike of the English reminded Wally of his own father who, railing against the English, would wag his finger at Edward the First, Hammer of the Scots, and mumble wistfully about the stolen Stone of Scone.

It was a mistake to think only old Scotsmen nursed such venom for England. Doyle was a young man and his anger was fresh and vital. Inside Doyle such intensity had a chance of being expressed, not just ending in smoldering bitterness as it had in Wally's father, Jock. Doyle could really be a warrior, built like the Earl of Kemble but with youth and quickness that would make him a favorite in any fight. A useful friend, perhaps, and Wally was short of friends just now.

"What's your business? Here in London, I mean." said Wally.

"I'm a medical student and I'm looking for a ship."

"Well that's a coincidence," said Wally. "Let me buy you a pint and we can talk."

The two of them sat outside the Mayflower pub, looking down at the Thames. Wally told Arthur—for that's how he preferred to be called—about his own medical training and his adventures on the *Bristol*. The young Scotsman's eyes sparkled as he listened to how Wally grappled with injuries and sickness on a ship at sea and how dope smugglers, pirates and bullies kept life interesting, to say the very least.

"That's exactly what I'd like to see and do," he said.

"It's not a picnic," said Wally.

"That's the point, isn't it? What's life without real adventure?"

"But you—you've got a home, a place in medical school, all the things I don't have."

"Wally, you don't understand. What I want more than anything else is to write. I love telling stories and making up adventures for my characters. But how can I create if I haven't seen something of the world? Edinburgh has only so many stories in it. I read everything I can lay my hands on, Oliver Wendell Holmes, Edgar Allen Poe, and, yes, Walter Scott, but I can't just spout back what they've come up with. It must be me that speaks."

"Well we are two sides of a coin, aren't we?"

"What do you mean?"

"We both want medicine and adventure. You have your medicine sorted out and now you're looking for adventure. I'm the other side of the coin, plenty of adventure but not enough medicine."

"What's it really like—being on a ship?"

Wally didn't answer at first. It had been weeks since he'd thought about life on the *Bristol*. He'd almost forgotten the long hours at night listening to the ship's timbers creak with each lurch through the sea, the ocean's rhythmic squeeze and release periodically interrupted by a wave crashing broadside on the hull. The adventure for a landlubber like Wally was in survival, in the daily surprise that such a flimsy vessel could withstand the oceans at rest let alone when they were stirred up by a storm.

"You get used to it. You really do."

"To what, though."

"I mean—the little things. They bother you at first, but you get used to them."

"Bad food, foul language—I can handle that," said Doyle.

"I was thinking more about being seasick and being lonely."

"I never get sick and I make friends with everyone."

Doyle certainly had the right attitude. He would be a very useful man to have on board, especially if he was good with his hands and could use a scalpel. The men would like him and that's half the battle in treating sailors. If they don't like the doctor then none of them will respond to his ministrations.

"Anyway, is London any better?" said Doyle.

"No, I suppose you're right." London was oppressive; its people couldn't be trusted; even the birds had left. "I should become a robber."

Doyle jerked his head around to look at Wally.

"What's that? I don't catch your meaning."

"Oh, I'm just a bit sour these days. I sometimes feel as if I'm just treading water, not getting anywhere."

"With your medical studies?"

Wally nodded agreement.

It might have been the second pint of beer or it might have been the sun briefly smiling at them through the sooty fog, but, whatever it was, the next hour saw Wally and Arthur busy chatting about their likes and dislikes, their pasts and their futures.

Doyle was a Catholic and had been to finishing school in Austria. He had already tried his hand at writing down some of the yarns he'd concocted but nothing of his had yet been published. He came from an artistic family, his father a painter who made a healthy income of two hundred and forty pounds a year, more than enough to support young Arthur all the way through medical school.

But Arthur wanted independence and was impatient to earn his own keep. He had thought about applying for the Queen's Shilling, the nickname, he explained to Wally, given to a soldier's pay, but the prospect of trekking across arid deserts in Rajasthan or chopping through thick jungles along the Congo didn't hold any appeal. Life aboard a ship sounded more leisurely and it carried with it the promise of a bunk, or at least a hammock, time to talk and read, and sea breezes carrying cool fresh air.

"Have you ever been on a boat?" said Wally.

"Well no, not yet."

"I thought as much."

"But I've read all about them."

"Reading? You think you can pick up what it's like by reading?"

"If the writer's honest and—"

Wally laughed. "Don't be silly. You've been listening to your own stories too much. Come with me tomorrow and we'll go down to Greenwich. The *Bristol* is docked there now and I'll ask some of the lads to show you around."

"You're on."

"But don't expect too much. The *Bristol* is a working ship, not an excursion boat, and every inch of space is geared towards moving cargo, not for basking in tropical sunshine and reading novels."

Arthur gave a sigh and shrugged his heavy shoulders. "I'm not the fool I look, Wally. Just take me down there. I'm keen to see the real thing—just as long as there are no dogs aboard."

"Dogs?"

"Oh, a fear of mine. I'll explain it to you sometime."

4 Doyle Signs On

The next day the two of them took the steam-ferry from Rotherhithe down to Greenwich. The tide was on its way out so the trip took less than thirty minutes. They disembarked at the passenger wharf and tramped along the south bank to where the *Bristol* could be seen lying off, at anchor.

The old barque looked asleep, so quiet and peaceful it rested, sails furled, its bow pointing up-river, looking towards the City. A little dinghy bobbed alongside like a duckling protected by its mother. A handful of men were at work on the deck, scraping and painting, their chortles and the smell of hot tar carrying across the water to Wally and his friend.

"Hey Stobber—Stobber!" Wally yelled to one of the group.

A tall, weather-beaten man with a scruffy beard detached himself from the others and shuffled to the rail. He waved over at them.

"Doc Wally. Is that you?"

"I've got a visitor. Can we come aboard?"

"Sure. Just a minute."

The tall man, Stobber Clucas, Manxman and first mate on the *Bristol*, dropped down the rope ladder that dangled over the ship's side, in the way old salts do, hands sliding down the rope and feet not even touching. He rowed the dinghy across to retrieve them.

Clucas, who'd been at sea for fifteen years, was an ideal guide for showing Arthur around a ship. He knew the way of ships inside and out, first from stories told him by his sailor father, then from working his way up the ladder from cabin boy to first mate on merchantmen roaming ports around the world. He'd survived typhoons and hurricanes, street gangs and pirates, cholera and the clap and he had a collection of scars, twisted knuckles and a glass eye to prove it. He could scamper up ice-bound rigging in howling gales and he'd make his men follow him to the top-trees, no matter how exhausted or how afraid the novices amongst them might be. The fact that he'd laid open a man more than once earned him respect, even with his masters.

Arthur was an eager student and he listened keenly as Clucas pointed out halyards, sheets and stays, clew lines, buntlines and braces and he asked questions about shipboard protocol for who was on watch when, when meals were served and what to call the captain.

"Poxy. That's what we call the old man, don't we Wally," said Clucas.

Wally's attention was elsewhere. He was scanning the ships anchored in this bend of the Thames. Instead of the wind-driven life they were designed for, here in the river they were just so many prisoners, manacled by chains and rodes to anchors or lashed to capstans or each other. There were barques, brigs, smacks and schooners, ketches, yawls, sloops and steamers, all in various stages of unloading or loading. Those about to weigh anchor were in the last stages of cargo trimming, the fine adjustment of a load to balance the ship on an even keel. Dockside cranes powered by noisy steam engines hoisted buckets of coal off Yorkshire coasters manned by dust-caked men from Cork, Glasgow, Cardiff and Jersey. The scene here, consistently crowded and noisy, mocked the romantic uncertainty of life at sea.

"Wally, a penny for your thoughts," said Arthur.

"Penny—what?"

"You were miles away," said Clucas.

"When'll you up-anchor?" Wally asked.

"In ten days, we head off to the Coast of Africa," said Clucas, his glass eye pointing east. "We take machine parts down and bring back copra, ivory and ambergris."

"How long'll you be away?" asked Arthur.

"Oh, six months or so. Depends on the weather. We'll do some trading along the West Coast before we get to Cape Town. Then we'll try to make it up to Zanzibar and Pemba—they've got good India rubber there, and cloves."

"I want to come," said Arthur, rubbing his hands together.

"Well, we'd have to talk to Poxy about that, but I don't see why not. We sure could use a surgeon down there. The bosun died from a machete wound last time I was down that coast—turned gangrene. 'Orrible sight, it was—and the stink …"

"I mean it. I do want to come."

Back in his cramped aft cabin, Percival Pockletree needed little convincing. The prissy little captain seemed thrilled to have a competent medical man aboard and, in his lisping high-pitched voice, he instructed Arthur to report back to the ship in five days time. Arthur would, of course, need to check out the dispensary, get his gear squared away and meet the men, all before the day they sailed.

"You'll learn the wopes quick enough when we put to sea," he told the young Scotsman.

Wally smiled. He had heard that understatement before, when he himself had joined the *Bristol* in New Zealand. But, back then, he had been more intrigued by the captain's lisp than the ship's ropes and rhythms. Time had changed all that.

"How will you sleep on a rolling bunk with a straw mattress when seas are sweeping the decks above you?" said Wally, lounging with his back to the ferry's wheelhouse, during their ride back to London.

"I believe I'll do just fine," Arthur replied.

"And when you're wet, lying in a leaky oilskin, exhausted and cold, sick to your stomach?"

"Nothing you say will put me off. You did it and from the look in your eye you'd give all your savings to go again."

Wally had no smart reply for that. It was the truth. He imagined all the interesting things he'd see in the markets—giant tortoise shells, hippopotamus teeth, rhinoceros horns and cowry shells—and all the various black people he knew so little about. He'd heard stories about the Kikuyu, the Ndebele, the Bantu and the Masai, but there must be dozens, maybe hundreds, of tribes all different in size and habits and language. Did they have the same loves and hatreds that the Maori had? How did they live? What did they think about the Europeans? It would be very interesting to walk amongst them. And how would they treat him, brown skinned man that he was?

Although it was summer a cold wind raked across the river. Seagulls hovered and wheeled above them and sooty smoke from the ferry's funnel swirled around them with every eddy or lull. Just as the

Thames was the historic entryway to the city of London it was also its major exit. From Greenwich a man could take his choice depending upon his fortunes and his mood, go west for London, industrial and overcrowded, or go east to the sea and a whole world beyond. Not everyone would see the choice that way but that's how Arthur saw it and so, most days now, did Wally. London was a place where you were anchored, a holding cell for boats and footloose adventurers. Every ship had a new destination planned—but did Wally? And how could he escape when Kemble held him captive?

Poxy had told Wally that his niece, Helen, was asking after him. She had given birth to a baby boy and planned to call him Walter. If only he could make it to Scotland, he thought? He could see her and they might have a future together.

5 Professor Moller

"Come and meet someone?" said Arthur, eyes bright and with a wide smile.

"Slack away your clewl'ns. Put some wind in your sails," he added, parroting phrases he'd just read in a Herman Melville books. His maturing as a sailor was proceeding at a fast pace though he hadn't yet embarked upon a ship.

"Who?" asked Wally.

"A short beat to windward, that's the tack we'll take."

"You're being annoying," said Wally.

"And you need some fresh air," answered the Scot. "That's if they call the air fresh these days over in Paddington."

A friend of one of Arthur's medical mentors taught at St Mary's Hospital Medical School near Paddington Station. It was an easy ride over there, on the Metropolitan subway train from Moorgate St, and they found their way to his laboratory, a cold windowless room in the basement. The air was heavy with the smell of furniture polish.

Augustus Moller, a short man with a neatly trimmed beard, was not much older than Wally or Arthur but he'd already established himself as an outstanding physiologist and teacher. He came from a medical family; his father was also a physiologist, so the curiosity of the scientist flowed in his veins. He was also very clever with building electrical instruments, the newest fad in experimental science.

"Here look at this," he said, beckoning Arthur and Wally over to a bench where copper wires coiled out from heavy batteries to a switchboard controlling lamps and lens-shutters poised over an open-chested rabbit. A flickering light beam that swung to and fro with each twitch of the rabbit's heart was projected onto a black screen making an eerie dance out of the rhythm of life.

"Beautiful, isn't it?" Moller said. With a tap of a switch he triggered an extra jerk of the rabbit's heart.

"See, I can cause contractions with each electrical stimulus."

"Did you use ether on the rabbit?" Wally had used ether as an anesthetic on the *Bristol*. He'd also seen a man die from inhaling too much.

"The animal's dead," said Moller. "I'm running the heart electrically." He punched out a rapid staccato on the switch and the light beam raced back and forward in response.

"If I come in too quick with an impulse, then nothing happens." Moller was talking out loud but he paid no attention to his audience, Wally, Arthur and a black bulldog sitting on a chair next to a desk.

"What's your dog's name?" said Wally.

"I call it the refractory period."

Arthur winked at Wally, and shrugged.

"I was asking the name of your dog," Wally said.

"Sorry. The dog? Jimmie."

"Good Scottish name," said Arthur. "Tame, I hope."

"It prevents the heart from developing tetany."

Wally raised his eyebrows and smiled. The scientist was apparently so caught up in his world of muscle twitching that he hadn't taken off his outdoor jacket: a navy pea coat with a heavy collar that could be turned up against frigid winds blowing in from the North Pole.

A book on the bench caught Wally's eye. Its title was *New Zealand, the Britain of the South* and a green ribbon bookmark stuck out from its middle pages. The last time he had seen that book was when he was a schoolboy. Back then it had been a source of annoyance for him with the patronizing way the author, a Mister Hursthouse, described the Maori. But now, on Professor Moller's desk, it looked more like an old friend.

"I see you're reading about New Zealand," said Wally.

"My sister's just moved there," answered Moller. "You're not from there, are you?"

"Yes, I am. I'm part Maori."

"Well, I'll be damned. You just might be able to help me solve a riddle."

Moller explained that his sister's husband had sent him clippings of New Zealand plants that were said, by the Maori, to have medicinal properties. However, being new to the country, the brother-in-law didn't know the names of the plants and had no idea of their supposed benefits. Now dried out and crushed during the four months voyage to England the specimens were probably fit only for the garbage bin.

Wally poked his finger at a clump of weedy-looking branches that held dark red and purple leaves.

"Well, this one is clearly *horopito*. You Pakeha—you Europeans—call it pepper tree. We soak the leaves in water, and then we use the water to bathe in if we have a skin rash. Some say the leaves can cure gonorrhea and stop a belly pain, but, frankly, I doubt it."

"And this one?" asked Arthur.

"I can't be sure, but it looks like *bidibid*. Look at the little spiny barbs. They can stick to a sheep in hundreds and spoil a whole fleece. We take the leaves and boil them, then use the juice as a tonic or for gonorrhea."

"Does everyone have the clap down there?" laughed Arthur.

"We never had it until the Europeans came. You brought it to us."

"Enough of that," said Moller, shaking his pen at the two of them. "Let's keep it civil. You sound like Gladstone and Disraeli, blaming each other for all the evil in the world."

"We wouldn't want to sound like politicians," said Arthur.

Moller slowly put his pen in the breast pocket of his jacket. "You speak as if you have some medical knowledge, Wally."

"Well, sir, I've had two years of training in New Zealand."

"With Millen Coughtrey?" Moller jerked backwards, putting one hand to his throat.

"Do you know him?"

The physiologist readjusted his jacket as if it was suddenly too tight. When he spoke it was with a quieter voice.

"He visited here, looking for a position in anatomy—before he took the job in New Zealand. Dunedin, isn't it? A very smart man, and I'm sure a good teacher. How's his school developing?"

"Well, there's been a lot of trouble …"

"Dammit, I have to be off. I have a class to teach," Moller said hastily. "Can you come back and see me late of an afternoon. Things quieten down by then. I'd love to hear more, Wally. You see Coughtrey is someone special to me. I'll tell you more next time." And with that he rushed off out of the room, his dog Jimmie, tagging along behind.

Arthur frowned at Wally "That's a bit weird. You heard what he said?"

"I wonder what he meant," said Wally.

"I think I know, and if I'm right your friend Coughtrey is a brave man."

Wally shook his head. Coughtrey was indeed a soldierly figure, bold and athletic, but how could Arthur know that, and how could Arthur understand Moller's cryptic comment?

"You must explain yourself, my friend," said Wally, now standing behind Moller's leather-backed chair, twirling in his fingers the white silk scarf that rested on its back.

Arthur paced slowly to and fro in front of the desk, his right hand massaging his forehead as if his deductions had caused a headache.

"Did anything about Moller strike you as odd?" he said.

"No. He's a bit potty, but so are a lot of teachers—even some doctors are on the weird side, all intense and preoccupied."

"What about his clothing?"

"What about it?"

"Well, the way he was wearing a jacket indoors."

"It's cold. This bloody basement never gets warm, I bet."

"And his collar up, like that? Didn't that strike you as odd?"

"No, why should it?"

Arthur paused and squeezed his lips together in a grim smirk.

"Well, my dear Wally, he was hiding something, that's why."

"What? What was he hiding?"

"If you'd taken the time to look more closely you'd have seen that the good Professor has a thick scar circling around his neck. When he's out walking he hides it with a scarf but indoors he keeps his collar up instead."

Wally let go of the white scarf.

"And, Doctor Sleuth, I suppose you know what caused the scar."

"It's absolutely typical of the deep laceration produced by the tight application of a garrote, an event, I might add, that's almost always fatal."

"Good grief!" Wally was now on his feet. "Do you really think that Moller was garroted?"

"Without a doubt, and if you'll permit me a small conjecture, I believe your man Coughtrey must have overcome the attacker, so saving Moller's life. As proof let me remind you, that when you mentioned Coughtrey's name, Moller's hand went right to his throat."

"Dammit, you're right. So it did."

For all of a week Wally and Arthur lived the high life in London. They toured the Tower of London and saw the Crown Jewels. They checked out the bustling Billingsgate fish market and explored the various meats on offer at Smithfield's. They listened to musical recitals at St Martins-in-the-Fields and they attended revues at the Royal and the Arcade. George Bernard Shaw had a new show on at the Haymarket so they took that in as well.

If there had been cricket played that week, or horse racing, they would have attended those as well.

"You said your dad is—was—a Scot. Right, Wally?"

They were walking down Pall Mall towards Buckingham Palace. Heavy clouds blocked the sun but at least it wasn't raining.

"Yes he was. He came to New Zealand for the whaling and he stayed."

"And your mother?"

"She's Maori—her name is Kirimoko. It means beautiful tattooed one."

"How extraordinary!" said Arthur. "I thought that intermarriage is ..." He paused, as if not sure where to take the sentence.

"Frowned on? Is that what you mean?"

"Well, yes, maybe that."

"My father saved my mother's life. It was something quite special."

"From what? What did he save her from?"

"I don't like to discuss it much," said Wally.

"You can tell me."

"He saved her from being murdered."

"Some tribal thing I suppose," said Arthur.

"No, a white man was about to kill her."

"Oh my god! And how did your father stop him."

"Let's not talk about it any more." Wally felt he'd already said too much. "And your background? You've not told me much about that either," said Wally, hoping to swing the conversation in a new direction.

"Not much to tell, really. I always felt more comfortable at school than at home. Friends I could talk to, that sort of thing."

"How interesting. Do go on."

"I started out at a Jesuit school—Stonyhurst—and ended up in Austria," said Arthur.

"Always wanting to do medicine?" Wally was pleased the focus had shifted from him.

"Well, no. I'm still not sure about medicine as a career. Might be a bit boring. I

couldn't sit and listen to old spinsters prattle on about their cats and their lost opportunities. Drive me bonkers, it would."

"I hadn't thought much about that side of things. I keep thinking about saving lives as a surgeon," said Wally.

"I thought about the army, of course."

"The Volunteers?"

"But to be shot in the belly in Africa didn't sound like a picnic either," said Arthur.

The reference to Africa reminded Wally about the box of bones in his dispensary when he was on the *Bristol*. Poxy's niece, Helen, was bringing them back to Scotland for burial.

"But, Wally, what about you?"

"Enough of me."

"I mean, how's your money holding out?"

"Good question, my friend. I'm pretty well skint." Wally had a habit of not addressing the big issues in a timely fashion. "And I was meant to have paid a man yesterday."

Wally hadn't told Doyle everything about his current circumstances. Some things were better left unsaid: his obligations to

Kemble, his gambling activities and his constantly living on the brink of poverty.

"Well, if you want a place at Edinburgh or Glasgow this year, you'd better look sharp about it, my man. Get a letter off, at least."

"I suppose I should." It was hard to be enthusiastic when he had so little money.

"Anyone would think you weren't interested," said Doyle. "But I know better. You just need some prodding."

"You're not in my shoes, Arthur." Everything looked so easy for Doyle, thought Wally, because he wasn't saddled with all the baggage of mixed blood, failed family and lack of fortune.

"Don't go off feeling sorry for yourself. Let's stop by old Moller again. See what he thinks."

They did go back to visit Moller. The professor seemed pleased to see them both and he entertained them talking about his friends at Cambridge. One highly-respected colleague was making new discoveries about the heart rhythms of the snail. Perhaps he would have a place for Wally in his laboratory. Snails seemed a long way from the clever surgery Wally had his hopes pinned on but he promised to think it over. As he listened to Moller he strained to see if there was a scar around his neck, one that could have come from an attempted garroting. Sure enough, there was a raised wheal of a scar mostly obscured by Moller's high collar, but unmistakable all the same. Wally's regard for Arthur Doyle's powers of observation was already high but this confirmation jumped it even higher.

That evening, Wally thought over what Doyle had said to him earlier in the day. He could work—it would be a struggle—on a letter of application to Glasgow. He'd been successful when he applied to medical school in New Zealand but this was a tougher assignment—famous university with lots of competition and with no powerful sponsors there to help him.

What could he say in such a letter? He could mention his time with Doc Chisholm, in the goldfields of Otago, when he was an apprentice of sorts. He'd spent two years in the new school in Dunedin, taking lessons from Professor Coughtrey, attending autopsies and watching operations. His time at sea would count for something, too, surely.

But on the negative side, the School in Dunedin had no reputation to speak of and he had no credentials from a British school or any local work experience. His time spent gambling would hardly count.

His pride wouldn't allow him to ask for help from Doyle or from Moller. He also knew that Kemble would be onto him quickly. He'd want his weekly payment. Wally had the two pounds but it was in his precious savings. There was no way he wanted to part with that now.

The only solution was to make a bigger stab at gambling. And where better to gamble than at Margate or Ramsgate, places where there'd be hundreds of vacationing suckers with fat wallets? The newspapers claimed that the summer season was in full swing and thousands of Londoners were soaking up all the local delights.

"I'll be away for a couple of days," he said to Doyle next morning at breakfast.

"Where to?"

"Margate."

"To play cards for money, I deduce."

Wally had not mentioned his gambling to Doyle so he was surprised to hear this answer.

"What makes you think that?"

"I've noticed you always carry a pack of cards in your jacket—De La Rues, I believe. You've never asked me to play so I assume the cards fill a more commercial function. You have some money but no job. You must then be a gambler, then. Correct?"

It was another accurate assessment from Doyle.

"Be careful, Wally," he added. "Margate is said to be a mite rough at night. I've heard that not even the porters at the Royal Sea Bathing Hospital are to be trusted."

"Oh, I will. And I'll be back Monday on the morning packet."

6 Margate

Margate was a working-class holiday town. In the summer its hotels were crowded with Londoners bent on having a good time. Children ate hard-boiled lollies bought off the pier and they flocked to the circus. Brave parents paddled in the water while more timid ones hired a bathing machine—a gaily-painted shed mounted on a horse-drawn carriage and taken into the water for the bather to immerse free from the leering eyes of onlookers. Organ grinders, fiddlers and minstrels made noisy music throughout the day and sing-a-longs and vaudeville recitals were held in music halls or at the bandstand each night. In whatever free time was left, the visitors scurried around an array of waxworks, shooting galleries, merry-go-rounds and peeping booths, the last of these featuring grotesque curiosities like the double-headed dwarf or the boy with hands that looked like lobster claws. The Promenade of Wonders offered a pipe-smoking monkey, an elastic-skinned man and an electric lady who emitted a shock to anyone who touched her. There were palmists, phrenologists, midgets and skeletons. The ladies paraded their finest clothes with bustles, bone-ribbed corsets, hats with feathers, and, for the cool nights, fur stoles and kid gloves. In truth, much of their finery was second-hand or borrowed; they hadn't the money to buy grand new clothes. Richer families took their holidays in the Lake District or, at the very least, in Brighton.

Wally left on the steam ferry; it sailed from Tower Pier at nine each morning. The usual throng embarked with him. On the way down to Margate everyone was in high spirits and not a few of them were already half-drunk. Working class people were not known for good manners and, with the prospect of a few days frolicking at the seaside, what few inhibitions they had were gone.

The less inhibited they are the better, thought Wally. If they're loose in their behavior, they'll be loose with their money as well.

He had two full days and nights to gamble. He'd taken two pounds from his reserves with Widow Murphy. This would be his bank to get him started. He had to make good this time.

At noon, he sauntered into The Empire Workingman's Club, an establishment whose most notable feature was its high-sounding name. He wouldn't have bothered to do so in London where the purpose of a workingman's club was to promote educational and moral improvement and to offer healthful recreation for its members. There, gambling was frowned on both by the club directors and by the law. But he'd heard the law was more elastic in Margate and other holiday towns. After all, a man had to let his hair down sometime.

He stood at the entrance and sized the place up. The Club was not much more than an old barn with twenty or so wooden trestle tables with benches scattered about. The rafters were bare and sparrows had nested up among them. But already the place was a-buzz with activity and as lively a Turkish bazaar. In one corner a dozen barmen served keg beer into big porcelain pitchers which thirsty punters carried about with them as they mingled. Conversations were conducted in a low shout and even then most of what was said was lost. A piano player struggled to make headway over the din created by a pair of Jamaican drummers and a tout bellowing the sale of raffle tickets. The air was filled with the smell of tobacco smoke, sweat and spilled beer. Cigarette butts and discarded sheets of newspaper were littered through the deep layers of sawdust that had been scattered across the floor. Not one woman was present. This was a workingman's home-away-from-home.

Wally took in a few stares, as he always did when he entered an almost totally white establishment. He'd covered up his tattoo but his brown skin marked him out as being someone different. He was better dressed than most, wearing his recently mended and freshly ironed shirt and his khaki trousers. Being a warm day, he carried his pea jacket over his shoulder.

Four tables of cards were already in progress. As usual, the most popular card tables were chemin de fer and baccarat but the crowd at the euchre table was noisy, laughing and half pickled. Wally counted at least ten pounds lying on the table. That's where I'll start, he thought.

Wally knew the game they were playing—*cut-throat*—and it amounted to having all three non-callers play against the man who called. The kitty, or pool, for each hand was shared out according to the number of *tricks* each player took. It was possible to have a winning day without ever having called once. Modest hands could be winners if a player outsmarted his opponents.

At times that day Wally was ahead; at others he was behind. The other players might've been tiddly but they were experienced and tightfisted with their money.

One man stood out—he wanted to taunt Wally. He was a little fellow but he talked more than the rest of the table put together. He had the look of a rat about him, with a pointed nose and jutting teeth—buckteeth. Instead of whiskers he had a toothbrush moustache and his swept-back hair was gingery brown.

"Ya scared, lucky lips?" He spat the words out of his sneering mouth as he raked in another of Wally's bets.

Wally tried to ignore him.

"Cat got ya tongue, darkie?"

Wally could feel his hackles rising.

"Aw, leave 'im alone, Freddy," another man said. "Let 'im blow 'is tanner." Sixpence—a *tanner*—was the largest bet Wally could afford.

"He's near busted anyways," added the irritating little fellow.

Wally bit his tongue. If he were to say something now it would surely lead to a fight and where would that leave him in his effort to regain his losses? A very few years ago he wouldn't have been able to resist throwing a punch at the little rat but he'd grown up a bit since then. His Maori mantras would have no effect on this hard-bitten crew and he was smart enough not to brandish his King Tawhai moniker. He knew that if it came to fisticuffs he'd be on his own; the other men would stick together like chewing gum.

By early evening, the sight of people around him eating meat pasties, fish and chips and sticky buns made him hungry. Not a morsel had passed his lips since breakfast. His two pound kitty was now down to ten shillings and without some food in his stomach he'd never be able to last out the night, the time when the other gamblers would start to fade and winnings would surely come his way.

He took his leave from the euchre table, giving Freddy the Rat a mock salute as he left. It made him feel superior to have held back from slogging him.

Outside the Empire Club the street was full of people. Some of the women wore large brimmed hats adorned with feathers or silks; they carried bright umbrellas and handbags on one arm and they linked their other with their man: husband, fiancé, pretty boy or mug. Whatever sun there had been was now gone, covered by coastal cloud. The men were wearing jackets and coats and Wally pulled his on as well.

He stopped at a horse-drawn cart where a man was selling local fresh fruit—tomatoes, apples and gooseberries mostly—and he bought a couple of green apples for tuppence. That was twice what he would have paid in London but it was cheaper than any meal he saw advertised on the windows of the cafes.

He strolled along to the jetty and mingled with the crowd gawking at street performers, jugglers and acrobats. Some of the performers were children and in their faces Wally saw pleasure. Their shirts might be torn or too small, they might have no socks or shoes, yet they were making do with what they had; they were independent. These youngsters inspired him to return to the tables, so he could be independent, too.

If only it was that easy, he thought.

The cards didn't fall his way that night nor did they on the next day either. Sure, a string of three or four hands might go well for him, but the net result was that he could barely muster the boat fare home on Monday morning.

On the boat ride back, he noticed his euchre nemesis, Freddy the Rat, was also on board. The cardsharp was deeply asleep, snoring, on a bench adjacent to the wheelhouse. His jacket lay carelessly on the planks beside him, almost inviting someone to filch from it. The invitation was too hard for Wally to resist. Had he not been so rudely mocked by the Rat, Wally would've listened to the soft whisper of his integrity. But poverty and desperation can bring on deafness.

He eased himself along the bench, making progress only when noise from the ships' engine or chattering passengers disguised his intentions. He watched the Rat closely for any wakefulness. It was

36

like sneaking up on a wild rabbit—the kind of sport he liked as a kid in Otakau.

The jacket was tweed with a herringbone pattern. It had probably once belonged to a gentleman, someone Freddy had fleeced, but now it was old and shabby, fit only for a hustler, a set of pockets for his winnings.

Wally gently gripped a sleeve and slowly tugged it toward him. It seemed almost too easy, at first, but the other sleeve was caught, lodged under the sleeping Rat. What was he to do? But the ferry lurched as it crossed another vessel's wake and the violence of the movement suddenly freed the pesky jacket.

Wally went aft and rifled through the pockets. There was a grubby handkerchief, a few sticky candy wrappers, a photo of an old woman in a smock, and a handful of loose coins —farthings, pennies, threepenny bits, sixpences and shillings, all adding up to nearly a pound. The excitement of his piracy was replaced by a guilty fatigue—an awareness of how little stood between him and a common street thief. Was this the way a fledgling doctor should behave, he mused?

He threw the offending jacket overboard and watched it settle lower and lower into the Thames until it finally sank beneath the ferry's wake, like a dead man never to be seen again but always to be remembered. The coins he put in his pocket.

The boat approached the dock and a tired Wally approached his moment of truth. He'd fallen behind in his obligation to Kemble, his only money was the meager profit of his thievery and the few pounds Widow Murphy had in hiding, and he still hadn't secured a position in any medical school.

He remembered something his old mentor, Doc Chisholm, used to say: it's better to be a living beggar than a dead emperor. But just then he wasn't so sure.

7 Escape

Arthur Doyle was waiting for Wally at the Tower ferry landing. He looked very concerned.

"What ya doing here?" Wally asked.

"You're in trouble, my friend."

"Keep your voice down. I mustn't be seen," said Wally working his way to the anonymous shelter of the ticket booth.

"You know then?"

"Know? Know what?" Wally whispered. He looked around for Freddy the Rat.

"A man called Kemble—his men—they came looking for you at Widow Murphy's."

"When?"

"Yesterday—last night. She said you were away."

"Oh God! Just what I need."

"Do you have their money? They claim you owe Kemble two pounds or more."

"Yes and no."

"Well, what are you going to do?"

"How do I know?"

"I have an idea."

Doyle suggested Wally take the train to Edinburgh, immediately. He could stay with Arthur's family until he found a suitable place at medical school.

"After all, you got me the job on the *Bristol*," said Arthur.

Wally quickly thought things through. It was a most generous offer, indeed, and the plan had a good chance of working. He'd have to escape without telling the Widow—Kemble's men would soon tweak it out of her if he did. They may be watching the house already.

And what did he have to lose. Nothing. He was half a Scot himself. Maybe he'd find himself at home up there. Clear air, clean water, birds chirping in the trees—just the thought of it made Wally excited.

"When does the next train leave?"

"At a quarter past the noon hour," said Arthur. "I checked myself this morning at King's Cross."

"I don't have a choice, do I?" said Wally.

Arthur nodded. He even gave Wally a shilling to help speed his way back to Widow Murphy's to pick up his belongings and his stored savings. It was already past eleven o'clock and there was no time to waste. For his part, Arthur would go directly to the station and buy a train ticket, so saving Wally precious minutes.

The hansom cab seemed to dawdle through the under-river tunnel that connected Wapping to Rotherhithe, but finally the boarding house came into view.

"I won't be a minute," Wally yelled back at the hansom cab driver as he bounded up the lodging-house steps, two at a time.

He jerked open the front door and called out "Hellooo!" There was no answer.

"Miss Murphy," he called, louder this time. Still there was nothing. She must be out, he thought.

Wally tried to figure out where the Widow Murphy kept his money? He'd seen her disappear into her bedroom with his safe-keeping, so he knew where to start. But who knows where she might hide it in there.

Luckily the door was unlocked. The blinds were down so it was dark and his eyes took a minute to adjust. He could smell her old-fashioned perfume. He saw the shape of a large bed, a tall-boy, a dressing table and a bedside table. Half-empty jars, pink powder puffs and glass atomizers stood crowded together on lace doilies with frilly edges. A silver frame held a photo of a newlywed couple, the man laughing and the woman, stooped, holding up a bunch of flowers in a gesture of surprise as if caught off guard. A corset was flung over the bedstead and coarse brown stockings lay in a heap in the corner with the walking stick she never used.

The obvious place to hide something was under the bed. He knelt down and looked into the dark recess beyond the shoes around the bed's perimeter. A large, ornate chamber pot was the first thing he saw. Something splashed out when he moved it but, more to the point, behind it was a cardboard shoe box. He eased the box out from behind the chamber pot and took off the lid.

His money was all there, the whole eight pounds and four shillings. He stuffed it into his pants pocket and hurried out of her bedroom.

Wally packed his belongings as quickly as he could. Into his sea bag went his spare pants, his blue shirt, socks, singlets, underpants and cutthroat razor. He loaded in *Quain's Anatomy*, *Syme's Clinical Surgery* and his *Edinburgh Dispensatory*. Time was too short to gather anything else. He looked at his watch. The train was leaving in less than fifty minutes.

He stumbled down the stairs, dragging his overstuffed sea bag behind him. Down the corridor he went, snatching an umbrella from the stand and his cap from the peg.

The sight of the front door slowly opening stopped him in his tracks. Too late to turn back, he raised the umbrella, ready to strike out at Kemble or his henchmen. They'd not stop him now.

"Wally, what are you playing at?"

The stooped Widow Murphy stood frozen in the doorway, a loaf of bread raised in self-defense. She looked like her wedding photo, the one Wally had just seen in her bedroom.

"Speak to me, boy."

Wally could feel the blood pumping to his face. How close he'd come to hitting the woman whose bedroom he just pillaged, whose bed he'd been under, whose chamber pot he had spilled. If not technically a robber, he was most certainly a cad, and her innocence of his actions made him feel even worse.

"I have to leave—now," he said, trying to edge past her. The little trolley she used for groceries blocked his way.

"You mean you're leaving?" she said.

"Please—I'm in a hurry."

"Is this all the notice I get?"

Wally fingers drummed on the watch in his pants pocket.

"Keep the deposit," he said, breathlessly.

"And what about your savings? I'll need to get my safety box."

"I'll write," he said, dragging his sack over her cart and rushing down the steps to the hansom cab.

41

"King's Cross, double-quick!" he yelled up at the driver. The cab didn't move.

"If I's to flog m'mare, she'll need an extra fare, guv'ner," shouted the cabbie in lazy Cockney singsong.

"A whole half crown if we make the station by noon," Wally replied, hoping his irritation was obvious even to this scallywag.

At the touch of the whip, the horse lurched off and sprinted down Tooley Street to London Bridge, the closest bridge to cross the river to get to King's Cross, but the cab slowed again to walking pace as it merged with the bustling bridge traffic.

Wally snapped open his watch. It was quarter to twelve. Monday was market day and street merchants were hawking their wares to anyone crossing the bridge. There were fishmongers, greengrocers, cobblers, peddlers and pawnbrokers, all wanting money from the wealthy patrons of hansom cabs crossing the bridge.

A dirty face looked in an open side window at Wally. "Apples ha'penny, dozen for fruppence."

"Bunch-o-flars for ya missus?" said another as he waved some weary poppies in Wally's face.

"Out of our way!" Wally yelled back at them.

"Damn you! Scoot! Scoot!" echoed the cabbie, swishing his whip at the scroungers, not wanting to lose the half-crown tip.

The gold filigree minute hand of Wally's watch moved faster and faster each time he looked and threading their way through the throng swept away five more precious minutes.

Wally's cab raced forward again through the City. St Paul's would chime at noon; Wally held his breath against hearing anything.

Unfortunately, the cab's route took him right past Kemble's office on Newgate Street. Nothing else for it, he'd just have to hunker down out of sight. But when the time came, he couldn't resist peeking out to see if he could spot his adversary. There was no sign of him at all.

The cab ground to a halt just as Wally heard the chimes of St Paul's, but they were still nearly a mile away from the station.

"What is it now?" called Wally, thumping his umbrella on the roof of the cab.

"Molly's 'ad it," was all the driver said.

The horse was down on its haunches, no strength left at all, an equine Pheidippides from Marathon. Molly had lost all will to proceed further and clearly another half-a-crown wouldn't make any difference.

Wally tossed the driver his fare and tip and jogged up Gray's Inn Road towards King's Cross. He was hot and sweaty and the sea bag was heavier than a load of bricks. His boots chafed at his ankles and more than once he nearly tripped on loose cobbles or bits of garbage. A mile at such a gallop and he'd know just how Molly the horse felt.

A couple of street urchins threw stones at him, laughing and jeering.

"Devil chase ya, Mister Wog?" one of them shouted. Out of wind and out of place, Wally gritted his teeth and pumped his feet, urging himself on and on. No matter how bad it hurt, it would be much worse if Kemble caught him.

No sooner did he reach the station platform than he saw the Earl. Drat! There were two other men with him, thugs by the look of them, both carrying bludgeons and God knows what else. One of the thugs held a sobbing boy by the scruff of the neck and the other was going through his pockets. Their attention seemed focused on their hapless victim but they were blocking Wally's path to reach the train for Edinburgh.

"Round here!" called a soft voice from behind the platform gate. It was Doyle. He beckoned to Wally to follow him. He led the way down the next platform and then cut back across the tracks and onto the Edinburgh train via a side-door he had left ajar.

"Smart, eh?" said Doyle, beaming from ear to ear.

"Very," said Wally, He leapt up the steps and into the carriage. "Just as long as Kemble's lot don't get on as well."

"They dinna buy a ticket, did they now?" Arthur said as he waved goodbye to Wally.

A loud whistle sounded and with a sudden shrug, the train started to move. Wally slid his watch out of his trouser pocket. It was twelve fifteen, on the dot. He smiled and, with his sleeve, he polished the image of blue sky, lake and mountains on the back of the watch case.

He looked up to see the fierce face of Kemble staring right through the carriage window at him. Stuck on the platform all Kemble could do was to shake his fist and mouth a curse. Wally replied with a casual wave, in the circumstances a more fitting taunt than any rude gesture a scoundrel might contrive.

8 Doyle Senior

The walls of Charles Doyle's Edinburgh studio in Lonsdale Terrace were lined with half-finished canvases, stacked three or four deep. The easel in the center of the room held a painting of a black horse, or at least the better part of the head and neck of a horse, which would be in the style of Stubbs if it were ever finished. Cigar ash littered the floor, as did blotches of brown and black paint. An empty whisky bottle sat alone in a corner, adding a further touch of gloom to all the paintings done in dark shades—no bright colors at all.

A desk with a mess of newspapers sat in one corner and above it was a sketching of a tall willowy boy wearing a Robin Hood hat and looking as if he had a headache. The boy was leaning on a golf club, looking more awkward than relaxed.

Beside the sketch a handwritten poem was pinned to the wall. The script was cursive and had the neat unhurried style of a child.

> *From birth to death, like tee to green*
> *Diverse trajectories of life are seen*
> *Some high and straight, some scuffed or curved*
> *Which ones are luck and which deserved?*

"Arthur's brother wrote that," said Doyle Senior, "just before he ..."

"Arthur didn't tell me he had a brother," said Wally.

"No, he probably wouldn't. He and Patrick never got along."

Wally wondered about the use of the word *never*. Where was Arthur's brother now and why had they never got along? He recalled the words of the old German schoolmistress he'd met in Penang: Never expect to quickly know the mystery of another. He thought he knew so much about Arthur, but large chunks of his life were still a mystery. He'd not even read anything of Arthur's writing.

"Did Arthur write poems too?"

"He was the storyteller. Liked to be the center of attention."

"He's got a keen eye for details," said Wally.

"Aye, but headstrong like his Mum. He always bucked authority, my own included."

Wally could see from the paintings that Doyle Senior's brand of discipline would be a harsh and dark one, enough to make a boy a boxer and to make him want to go to sea. Arthur must have welcomed the chance to spend his childhood at a succession of boarding schools. He wanted to ask more about Arthur's brother: his name and how old he was, for a start. But something about the older man's manner told Wally not to.

The Doyle house was nothing like Widow Murphy's. It was quiet for one thing, and it didn't smell of burnt bacon or boiled cabbage. The floors were wood and polished and the curtains weren't torn or dirty.

Mrs. Doyle was a tall lady with full strong features, like Arthur. She'd made Wally welcome but that was about all. She was clearly not one to waste words on small talk and Wally had only one big item on his mind.

His urgent business was to visit Edinburgh's distinguished old hospital on Infirmary St and see Dr Bell, a kind man, according to Arthur, who might be able to suggest useful medical contacts in Glasgow. But Arthur had also cautioned Wally that Bell was something of a trickster in conversation and for Wally to be on his guard. He was a brilliant clinician and something of a hero for Arthur. Doyle Senior made the arrangements for Wally's visit.

Bell's office was in the main building, a four story brick edifice with a high turret towering over the main entrance. The building had seen better days and plans were afoot to see it knocked down in the near future. From the quadrangle in front, a visitor could see broken slates on the roof and mossy growth sprouting from cracks in the walls. Wally's appointment was for two o'clock.

"Arthur says you've been to sea," the doctor offered as an opening gambit. He wore a heavy jacket and his gas fire was turned up high even though it was summer.

"I came all the way from New Zealand," said Wally.

"And did you see any giant squids or sea serpents?"

"No sir, nothing other than a few little octopuses swimming around in a tank in a market in Penang. But perhaps if I'd sailed by Thimble Tickle …"

"And no sea serpents, either?"

"I read somewhere that the crew of one of Her Majesty's ships recently spotted a giant finned serpent near Sicily, something like your own Loch Ness monster, I believe. But no, I never saw such a thing." Wally wasn't comfortable with this line of questioning. He had his own superstitions, Maori ones, to deal with and he hadn't quite decided whether to believe in giant sea monsters or not. He couldn't figure out where the wily old teacher was leading him.

"Then it's all poppycock, don't you think?"

"These sightings, sir? What those men reported?"

"Yes."

"Well, they may well believe they saw something of the kind, but I'd need better evidence to be convinced myself." Wally had the feeling that Dr Bell was moving into the realm of philosophy. Was this what Arthur warned me about, he thought?

"Evidence? Evidence? What sort of evidence?" The man's face looked gruff and unfriendly. He might've been playing a role, but he also might have been offended at something Wally had said. Whatever could it have been?

The room didn't feel chilly any more. Wally felt sweat forming on his upper lip and across the top of his forehead. He must think of something—and quickly!

"A photograph might be sufficient proof."

"A photograph can easily be faked. No, that wouldn't be proof for me," said Bell.

"Well, a specimen, then—a piece of a fin or a tentacle."

"Same risk! Could be bogus. Could come from anywhere."

This grilling was like a viva voce examination, the oral testing that medical students were forced to endure. Wally knew there was a right answer and Bell wouldn't be of any help unless Wally came up with it.

"An autopsy, sir. That would be the clincher, wouldn't it?"

"Top marks, young man! Damn sure it would."

From then on, the interview went smoothly. There had been a bizarre logic to Bell's interrogation. A coroner friend of his in Glasgow, Dr Archibald Hackshaw, needed a skilled mortuary assistant. It was a paying job but needn't be full time. If Wally wanted it, the job could be his. Talk about falling on his feet. Wally was very pleased.

He ambled over to the High St and then across the North Bridge to Princes St. Everywhere the names on the metal street signs reminded him of Dunedin. Here there was a plaque that said George St, another for Queen St and, a little further along, there was a Heriot Row. Homesick early settlers in Dunedin had tried to recreate another Edinburgh by using these same names in the south of New Zealand but, in so doing, they had distorted the very memories they were trying to preserve. For them, Princes St now lacked a grand castle with stately bordering gardens and Dunedin's muddy tracks and quagmires stood in for Edinburgh's neat cobblestones and macadam.

For Wally, any sense of déjà vu was reversed. The names were familiar but the streets were strangers to him, like unknown ancestors of childhood companions. But would his hometown streets now feel as foreign as these in Edinburgh?

Mrs. Doyle said nothing when Wally broke the news that he would leave for Glasgow the next morning. Her blank expression would be of use in poker, Wally thought, but not much help in mothering two boys, which raised again the question of where was Arthur's brother.

"Will Arthur's brother be home for dinner, tonight?" he asked.

"No." Her face remained unmoved.

"Is Patrick not living here just now?" said Wally, eager to drag almost any information out of the reticent Mrs. Doyle.

For her part, she simply walked out of the room and plodded her way up the staircase. The only communication she gave to Wally was in her eyes—she looked at him as if he had struck her with his fist.

She wasn't present at dinner that evening but Doyle Senior was and he explained his wife's mysterious behavior.

It seems that Arthur's brother had been the victim of a tragic accident almost ten years before. The family had been on holiday in the West of Scotland, living in a little farm cottage out on the moors.

It was an idyllic place, with high mountains behind and a wonderful view out over the fields of wild flowers that filled the valley. One night, Patrick had taken it into his head to wander away from the cottage, possibly to spy on the rabbits that frolicked around the vegetable patch beside the nearby stream.

No one had warned the Doyles that a vicious hound, a mastiff, had been terrorizing the farms in that area, killing livestock and threatening the residents.

When Patrick was found missing from his bedroom in the morning, a search was started and, before long, his savagely-mauled lifeless body was found, lying in a heap, in the vegetable patch just a few yards from the stream.

"Oh, I'm so sorry," said Wally. He felt badly about bringing it up.

"You were not to know," said Doyle Senior.

"Arthur never told me anything about that." Yet, Wally remembered, he did admit to a fear of dogs.

"No, he wouldn't. He has never come to terms with the death of his brother—none of us have, I suppose. We all have to learn to deal with things in our own way, and I expect Arthur is working on his own response."

"Maybe that's why he wants to go to sea, to have time to think and recover."

"Maybe—but it's just as likely he needs time to decide whether medicine is what he wants to do in life. After what happened to Patrick he may not want to be around any more gruesome scenes. And as for children suffering ..."

Wally could see the sense of that statement. He'd seen the way his father avoided life after the sorry episode where he'd killed a man to save Kirimoko.

Dark events play havoc with the mind. His biggest surprise was that he hadn't suspected that Arthur might have lived in such proximity to tragedy. Much about Arthur, about anyone for that matter, was hidden from view.

And now, Wally was off to Glasgow to try again to complete his medical degree and, of all things, to work in a big city morgue where he'd see all the decay and despair of a coroner's investigations.

Like it or not, he would get to see a lot of things that were hidden from others' view.

9   The Mortuary

Archibald Hackshaw was a fussy fellow, both in manner and dress. He had trained as a surgeon under the great man Lister but because of administrative squabbles about Listerian methods he had been re-assigned to the mortuary, doing autopsies on coroner's cases—deaths with suspicious circumstances.

"We have a serious duty here," he told Wally when they sat down together for the first time. He pressed the palms of his hands together as if in prayer and he looked at Wally over the top of horn-rimmed spectacles that made him look older than his forty-five years.

"Our first obligation is to the deceased," he continued, "to see that any wrong done to them is exposed. But we must also pay service to the townspeople by ferreting out diseases that might be contagious."

"Oh I like detective work," said Wally, with a smile he hoped looked eager.

Hackshaw put on a serious frown that said lightheartedness was not welcome in his mortuary.

"Wasn't so long ago we had grave robbers and body snatchers here in this very city," said Hackshaw. Wally had read the lurid stories of the resurrectionists, as they were called, stealing fresh corpses to sell to medical schools for anatomic dissection. Some poor wretches had even been killed to provide fresh subjects for study. He thought of his own mother who had come so close to being murdered by Grigor Clucas, all for the sake of selling her tattooed head to some sick London ghoul.

"Many of our children live in slums and hovels, brothels and coal-cellars. They live as thieves, pickpockets and prostitutes. It's them we need to avenge when they end up here. Follow what I'm saying?"

"Yes sir, I'll be worthy of the task."

"Well, I hope so," Hackshaw said as he rose from behind his wooden desk. "Now let's get started."

It didn't take long for Wally to learn the routine. The mortuary was swabbed out every morning and evening, like an operating room or, as Wally observed, like the deck of a well-serviced ship. A technician sometimes helped but Wally did most of the work, from sharpening knives to sawing through ribcages. He weighed each organ as it was removed and entered notations in the autopsy record. The sewing-up was left to him as well.

Over the weeks, Hackshaw's attitude softened and he championed Wally's admission to the medical school. An arrangement was worked out where Wally worked in the mortuary in the mornings and he attended classes in the afternoon. His stipend was sufficient to cover his boarding expenses in the medical school hostel and he had enough to salt away a few shillings every month as well. As poor as Wally had been, he now felt well-to-do.

During the detailed explorations of the bodies brought in for examination Hackshaw often talked about his days as an assistant to the great surgeon Joseph Lister. He was a *dresser*, a term in use for centuries which referred to the practice of the junior member of a surgical team having the responsibilities to dress the patients' wounds. His associates from that time, Hector Cameron and William Macewen, were now practicing surgeons at the Glasgow Royal Infirmary and they continued Lister's controversial new methods of antisepsis, keeping the operating room and wards spotlessly clean and lavishing carbolic acid on all and sundry to discourage putrefaction.

Hackshaw came to treat Wally as a student, the kind of pupil he still wished he had, and would've had, if he'd not been kicked out of the Infirmary.

"See how I can access the esophagus from below the diaphragm," Hackshaw might say, pulling the stomach of the cadaver down into the abdominal cavity. "A tear in the lower part can be repaired with such an exposure."

"Here, look at the size of this ovarian tumor. We can lop off a bit and look at it under the microscope. Malignant, without a doubt."

"The knife entered his aorta here, don't you think? And you can see where the blood gushed out. Not something you'd want to do in surgery, is it Wally?"

He supervised Wally practicing sewing up different incisions and he explained how best to suture pieces of bowel together and how to repair a fistula.

Wally's dexterity with a scalpel and needle was soon noticed in the hospital, and he was invited to spend more and more time in the operating rooms. Of the surgeons, it was William Macewen who became Wally's favorite. Much of the work he did was in repairing congenital abnormalities of children's joints. It was painstaking work requiring a lot of chiseling of bone as well as meticulous steps to avoid infection. He also worked on abscesses and tumors of the brain, intestines and lungs and whatever else was presented to him. He loved showing off his exceptional prowess in the most complex extirpations and excisions and Wally became an eager admirer.

Macewen's patients were in awe of the man. His physical stature was imposing, his voice booming and his disregard for administrative timidity legendary.

Wally spent a lot of time in the long dormitory wards at night preparing patients for the surgery next day. He developed a friendship for many of them but none more so than for Jeanie Campbell, a young prostitute, who had been admitted for a severe infection that ravaged her body after a back-street abortion.

Jeanie shuddered with chills each time her temperature climbed and she collapsed in sweaty exhaustion when it fell. At the fever's height, when the thermometer read one hundred and five, her face seemed painted red, an effect enhanced by her ginger hair. Macewen judged her condition to be too precarious for him to operate, so all she had was the meager comfort of cold compresses and watered-down lemon juice.

Wally would sit at her bedside holding a mug to her parched lips and offering a sympathetic ear as she mumbled through her deliriums.

Each day there would be an hour or two when she was quite coherent and it wasn't long before their talk grew to include life outside the Infirmary.

"What brought you here, Dr McConnochie?" she asked.

"I'm not a doctor yet, Miss Campbell, but I hope soon to be. You should simply call me Mr. McConnochie—or Wally, if you like."

"Well then, Wally, I'm not often called Miss Campbell. Jeanie's my name. Please use that."

"And a nice name it is."

"You haven't answered my question."

"About why I'm here?"

"Yes." She wiped her face with a wet cloth and dabbed the corners of her eyes.

"To study—to become a surgeon. I want to make people better."

Jeanie gave a sigh. It made her sound like an old lady, someone who'd tired of hearing life's platitudes.

"Sure, I used to be like that three or four years ago. But now, I'm ..."

"Don't listen to yourself. You're sick! Life will seem brighter when you're cleared of this fever."

"Thanks for your kindness, Mr. Wally, but I know how to be honest with myself and I know what's in store for me. There's no brightness in my future."

"I'll be here with you."

"That's something. Thank you."

Each day they would talk about something new. Jeanie described the life she lived on and off the streets of Glasgow. Most of the time she was under the patronage of wealthy older gentlemen, men with enough money and time to afford a mistress as well as a wife. Some of her patrons were mixed up in the darker side of big city life: blackmailers, smugglers and confidence tricksters. A few merited being called thugs and more than one was a murderer. Jeanie never broke their confidence by saying their names but Wally guessed at their identities when he observed her steady stream of admirers at Visiting Hour each evening. Pinstripe suits, bow ties and polished boots spoke for their money and heavy fists, broken noses and perpetual scowls attested to their thuggery. One was said to be a City Councilman, others were financiers and barristers.

Her most frequent visitor wore a clerical collar but his hushed words were not prayers.

"He'll be pleased when I'm gone," Jeanie told Wally later.

"Oh, don't say that! You're not going anywhere—and who ever would be pleased?"

"He's not the only one. You don't know the half of it, Wally."

"Well, I do know—"

"No, you don't. That double-faced hypocrite sounds so pious and saintly at his church on a Sunday but the rest of the week he's breaking every rule in the book—all in secret, of course. And that's his worry—that I'll spill the beans to the Bishop or write a letter to the paper. That'd do him in."

"And would you?"

"No. Why bother? Even if did, the Bishop wouldn't take my word against one of his own. And I've never learned how to write, have I?"

Wally's stories about himself seemed tame by comparison or so he thought. But Jeanie listened closely to each of them, as long as her fever held at bay. He talked about his childhood on the Maori *marae* in southern New Zealand, at Otakau, and how he later lived with his parents at Logan Point on the northern side of Dunedin's harbor. He told her about horse riding, fishing, hunting rabbits with a rifle and hiking over the hills to collect mushrooms. He recounted legends his mother told him as a child and he shared some of the tales told him by sailors on the *Bristol* during quieter times on the long voyage over to Britain.

Jeanie's parents had lacked for happiness, she told Wally. They constantly bickered and bitched and their hostility for each other left little affection, and often little food, for Jeanie and her younger sister. The last straw was when they both took off, leaving the girls alone and neglected. For three days, Jeanie, still only twelve years old, and her sister struggled to manage for themselves until neighbors intervened and took them to the convent. The nuns took care of them both for the next four years.

"What a horrible time for you and your sister."

"No, not really. At least there was no fighting—and we were treated like little princesses."

"But what happened then?"

"I decided I'd never go hungry again and I'd always be independent. The way I chose has allowed me both."

"You have my admiration," said Wally.

"If only I had some of your health—that's the one thing I didn't think about," said Jeanie.

55

"And your sister. What's become of her," said Wally.

"She's a nun and teaching school in Hong Kong. Still dependent, I suppose you could say, but at least she's never hungry."

10 Kemble Again

Eventually Kemble showed up. Wally spotted him quizzing the Assistant Matron at the main entrance to the hospital. He ducked down a side hallway before the Earl could see him. There's no escape from that man, he thought. How did he track me here?

Wally tried to muffle his loud breathing as he peeked around the corner. He saw Kemble waving his arms about and he heard his angry rebuke as he stormed off: Damn the rules!

When the coast was clear, Wally went to the Assistant Matron and asked what Kemble had wanted.

"He was enquiring after your whereabouts, doctor." The Assistant Matron, an old crone as diligent as any sentry, would know full well where Wally lived but hospital rules forbade giving out such information to strangers.

"And did you tell him?"

"What ya take me for? Mind you, his shilling did look tempting." As well it might to someone who always looked at Wally in a disapproving way, as if he smelled uncivilized or might at any time exhibit some vulgar native behavior.

"Was he upset?"

The Assistant Matron frowned and looked away.

"Well, was he?" Wally persisted.

"He called me a rude name," said the old woman, turning to look directly at Wally. "And he said you were a no-good wog."

"Well, thanks for not saying anything," said Wally. "Did he tell you where he was staying?"

"Oh yes. He's said he'd be at the Grosvenor, up on Queen St. Till the weekend, that is. His business would be done by then, he said." The Assistant Matron's manner was more civil than usual, as if someone else calling Wally a wog had cleared the air between them, especially as he didn't seem bothered by the insult.

That night, Wally told Jeanie about the Earl of Kemble and the devilish scheme that he had fallen victim to. He explained the risks to life and limb he'd incurred by not answering to his debt.

"Why not just pay him back and be done with it?" she asked.

"I don't have that kind of money."

"How much is it?"

"Fifty pounds, by now, I bet. Once he calculates up all his interest and expenses."

"Let me pay it for you," Jeanie offered.

"No, that would never do. Don't even say something like that. It wouldn't feel right and the Dean would have my guts for garters. Macewen would too."

"I know the Grosvenor," she said. "A pretty place, with a fine view of the castle."

The next few days, Wally was on edge. His progress to and from the morgue and hospital was as furtive as a cat traversing a dog pound. He checked out every street before he stepped into it and he paused at every doorway along the way. He asked the Assistant matron if Kemble had been seen again and he scrutinized the faces of all his acquaintances for signs of treachery.

Not hearing or seeing anything of Kemble for three days, Wally brought the matter up with Jeanie.

"Oh, don't worry your head about it," she said, smoothing her bedspread and flicking away imaginary crumbs. She hadn't eaten a thing for a week.

"That easy for you to say," said Wally. "It's not your neck he's after."

"I'm sure it'll all work out just fine."

"Yeah, sure."

"Can you let me rest now, Wally? I'm a little fevered tonight."

"Aren't we all?"

Wally walked away out the doorway of the ward. He wished he hadn't been abrupt with Jeanie but she just didn't understand what a pickle he was in. She'd obviously flirted and conned her way out of many tricky situations in the past but it wasn't as easy for a man, and a poverty-stricken brown one at that.

An hour in McTaggert's pub helped ease some of his frustration. Scottish beer was as fine as any served in London and a site better than the limpid swill that was passed off for the real thing in New Zealand.

When he entered the morgue next morning, the first person he saw was Sandy, the technician. That in itself was odd because the lazy old fellow liked to hide away in the formalin room pretending to mix solutions while Wally did the heavy work setting up the first cadaver on the big wooden block table.

"Let me do the honors this morning, Wally." Hard to believe, he seemed to have an eager attitude to match.

"Why? What's gotten into you, my friend? Who'll mix the fixative?"

"Oh, I got plenty for now." The man's unaccustomed readiness to help made Wally suspicious.

"Why? What's up?"

"Nothing. There's nothing."

Wally was now certain something was up. "Shouldn't I check with Hackshaw?" he said.

"No. He's the one what told me to tell you."

"Because?"

"Because you know the deceased!"

The news hit Wally like an icy splash. There aren't many people that I know, he thought. Could it be Macewen? Surely not—he was as fit as any man. Might it not be Kemble? Oh yes, that rogue has finally met his comeuppance. It must be him.

"I think I know who it is—and it wouldn't bother me to see the scoundrel laid out on the block. Not in the slightest! He's had it coming."

"It's not a he, sir. It's a she."

"She?"

"Yes, Miss Jeanie Campbell. Dr Hackshaw says you know—knew—her pretty well, if you'll excuse the expression, sir."

Wally felt his stomach lurch. The room seemed to be spinning. All he could think of was that he had to see Jeanie again. He had to tell her how sorry he was that he hadn't been able to help her. He hadn't even been able to stop her fevers, let alone save her life. To not see her again would be horrible—it would only double his pain.

In a fog of emotion, part sadness, part anger, Wally rushed in to see Dr Hackshaw. The coroner was sitting at his desk, as he always was early in the day, reading the newspaper.

"Dr Hackshaw!"

"Yes, Wally."

"What's this about my not being needed this morning?"

"Did Sandy not tell you? One of your patients is here."

"Well, that's even more reason for me to help out, isn't it?"

"Usually, yes of course. But the young lady left specific instructions that you were not to be present at any - what did she call it?—*post-mortual exploration*. That sounds like an autopsy, don't you think?"

"Why on earth not?"

"It's too late to ask her, Wally. All I can suggest is that you take it up with Bill Macewen. He's the one who reported her instructions to me."

Wally had no more words to say. He hid his face in his hands. He didn't cry, but he came close to it.

Wally hurried over to the operating theaters. Macewen was in the Surgeons' Lounge, having a cup of tea between cases. He smiled when he saw Wally hurry in.

"Fine morning out there, Wally."

Wally paused to catch his breath and to compose himself. After all, Macewen was his mentor and the master of his fate, at least with respect to his making it as a surgeon.

"Sir, could you please tell me why I cannot see her."

"*Her* being Miss Campbell, I presume."

"Yes."

"Well, young man, that's what she wanted."

"You mean you talked to her about it, sir?"

"Yes, last week. She knew she was going to die soon. We talked about it. Said you meant the world to her. Said she wanted you to remember her as she was when she was alive, that sort of thing. You know."

"I meant the world to her?"

"That's what she said."

"But I—we—did nothing to help her."

"*We* did all we can, Wally."

"But it wasn't enough."

"It often never is."

The older man drained his teacup and put it down on the side table and picked up his surgical mask. He started for the door that led to the operating theaters, but turned again to face Wally.

"The best we had to give, Wally, was comfort. And that is what you gave. Don't ever underestimate the importance of giving solace to your patients. Now, come along and scrub in on this next case with me. It's a brain abscess in a young boy from Paisley and I'll let you do the drilling."

Macewen's words helped Wally simmer down and he wandered off to find his surgical apron. The thought of Jeanie lying alone on the mortician's marble slab still stung, but he had meant the world to her, and maybe Macewen was right. Maybe he had been a help to her when she needed it. She didn't really need him now.

A few days later, at Jeanie's funeral, Wally was surprised to see that the minister conducting the service was the cleric who'd visited her regularly in hospital—an old customer and a hypocrite she'd called him. He was even more surprised when the minister signaled to him, beckoning him over.

"There's something I should tell you, Doctor."

"It's Mister. I'm not a doctor yet."

"Well, Mister then. It has to do with keeping your mouth shut."

"Oh, yes?" said Wally, a bit taken aback by the minister's direct way of speaking.

"You see, on the instructions of Miss Campbell I paid off a note you owed to an Earl Somebody-or-other."

"Kemble? You paid off Kemble?"

"Yes, that was his name. Fifty five pounds, I paid him."

"That's wonderful of you." Wally could hardly believe what he was hearing. He could be free of Kemble and his henchmen forever. "But why would you do that?"

"You see, I would prefer it if you never mentioned that I was a special friend of Miss Campbell. Not to anyone. Understand? Not to the Bishop, not to a priest, not even to a bloody church mouse."

"I understand," said Wally.

"She said you would. And, in return, she told me to give you Kemble's receipt."

The minister handed Wally a faded yellow docket on which a set of numbers had been over-written with Kemble's signature and the words paid in full.

11 Graduation

The next year, Wally's final year at the University of Glasgow, was a busy one. There was so much to learn just about the care of children—a sore throat was probably simple tonsillitis but it could also be diphtheria and turn fatal. An anxious mother, fearing the worst, needed a confident doctor if his reassurance was to be believed. Obstetrics also took up a lot of time. Many children died at birth and woe to the practitioner whose manner suggested he might have prevented it if only he were more expert. Then there were all the infectious diseases that ravaged the city. Typhoid and tuberculosis he knew about but appendicitis, quinsy and erysipelas were new to him.

Scurvy had been bettered with limes and lemons but no such cure was known for rickets, goiter or wet gangrene. The art of dealing with such mystery diseases was subtler and more demanding than if their cause was known. A good physician had to look as if he had the answer even when he didn't.

Perhaps that's why Wally preferred his time in surgery: the scalpel is decisive and the scar evidence of something definitely done.

Nearly every hour was devoted to learning his craft. He had no thoughts for travel, and his letter writing was meager, not that there were many people for him to bare his heart.

To his mother, Kirimoko, he wrote about life in Scotland, but he knew she'd heard all about wondrous Caledonia before, ad nauseam, from Jock, her husband. What's more, she couldn't read, so each letter had to be read aloud to her by Wally's old girl-friend, Kotuku. It was like writing to both at the same time. New Zealand was so far away and it took months for their replies to reach him. He didn't write them very often.

He knew he had uncles and an aunt living no more than a dozen miles away in Ayrshire but he always found an excuse not to seek them out. What interest would they have in him? What on earth could he talk to them about? There'd be so much explaining to do: his color, his tattoo, his leaving his mother alone in New Zealand. Why bother seeking out long-forgotten relatives of his dead father just to be poked and prodded like some circus curiosity? Hadn't he traveled halfway around the world to escape the reproachful looks cast on him by white-skinned Pakeha socialites? Better they not know he's here. Let's not challenge their prejudices or, worse, confirm them.

A couple of times, he sent a little note to Helen—he was shy about saying too much—and reinforced his promise to visit, but it would be after graduation. Her manner was so chummy that he was nervous about writing more often.

Doyle was his most frequent correspondent. From him, Wally heard about his time in Africa aboard the *Bristol*, the excitement of canoe trips up dark rivers in Sierra Leone and Nigeria to barter with unpredictable natives and visits to remote sandy islands off the coast of Mozambique populated only by noisy grey parrots and green lovebirds. Wally promised to visit him and hear more as soon as his examinations were over.

All year the prospect of his final examinations hung over him like a dense fog, not unlike the smoky haze that settled on Glasgow that winter. Coal fueled the factories, the steam trains and the kitchen stoves. Vile black clouds belched out of chimneys, smokestacks and funnels as far as the eye could see, though even when it wasn't raining that wasn't more than a mile or two.

The examinations were held over a week in May. Written papers were followed by oral interviews, so-called *viva voces*, and the nervous students were quizzed at the bedside of patients who displayed classic signs of unusual afflictions. The toughest part was the oral test in medicine, always held on the last day, and the sternest examiner was Dr Archibald McLeish, a big-boned and ruddy-faced man with grey muttonchop whiskers.

McLeish, now near retirement, had been born in Demerara in British Guiana, the son of a sugar planter, and it may have been there that he developed a dislike for colored people. Scarcely a week went by without another story of his high-handed rudeness towards an African, an Indian or a Jamaican. In lectures or in clinics, he had never commented on Wally's brown skin, but who knows how he might react if he were in the omnipotent role of final examiner, the man with the power to make or break Wally's hope of becoming a doctor.

Another factor might also conspire to arouse McLeish and that was Wally's clear preference for working with Macewen, a man who outshone McLeish both personally and professionally. McLeish's envy might light the fuse to blow Wally's chances away.

Wally might have been paired with any one of a dozen other examiners but, as luck would have it, it was McLeish who beckoned him in when he knocked on the examination room door.

"Name?" snapped McLeish.

"McConnochie, sir. Walter McConnochie." Wally knew full well that McLeish knew his name.

"Well, my aboriginal friend, we finally get to talk." It was not a promising start but Wally kept a straight face. He concentrated on the old physician's eyes, the way a prizefighter does when he tries to sense an upcoming punch. McLeish's were narrowed and twitchy and he seemed to be staring right back.

"A pleasure, sir. It's a pleasure to be here."

"Well, we'll see about that, won't we?"

The senior physician preened the lapels of his white coat and jerked his head towards a young man who occupied a chair in a far corner of the room.

"Mr. McConnochie, I want you to examine this gentleman and tell me what you find. You're not to put any questions to him, but you may instruct him to perform appropriate clinical maneuvers."

"Certainly."

"You may call him Jenkins."

"Good morning, Mr. Jenkins." Wally extended his hand in greeting and was surprised that Jenkins withheld his. "Would you be so kind to sit up here on the examining table? I'll be poking and prodding you a little bit, and I may ask you to do certain things. None of them should be too difficult."

The patient grunted an acknowledgment and shuffled his bottom onto the examining table. He'd probably done this many times before, in other years, with different students.

Not having any history to go on made things very difficult. How was he to focus in on the man's problem? It could be anything from the top of his head to the tips of his toes. He stroked his chin and tried to think.

"Come on then, man. Stop dithering about." McLeish was needling him.

"If only I had one or two things to—"

"You darkies are all the same! Want to be led by the hand, don't you?"

The patient, the man they were calling Jenkins, gave a little smile as if he'd just heard a joke. McLeish suddenly looked flustered and not a little irritated and he signaled for Jenkins to keep a straight face.

Wally thought back to what McLeish had said. Something in his words had amused Jenkins. Was it the part about darkies all being the same? Wally had heard that insult many times before, and he assumed Jenkins probably had heard it too. Or was it the part about being led by the hand? Was that why the man had not joined him in a handshake? Had McLeish made a slip-of-the-tongue and given him a vital clue?

"I certainly don't wish to be led by the hand, sir." He watched Jenkins closely and, even though the patient tried to suppress it, there was a little flicker of a smile around his eyes.

Wally said to Jenkins, "Could you stretch you arms out in front of you, sir?"

The man obliged, and when he did, both hands hung limply down.

"Could you hold your hands out straighter, please?"

"I can't sir. That's a big part of me problem, I can't straighten—"

"No talking, Jenkins. Hear me! No talking."

But Wally now knew he was dealing with a nerve problem causing wrist drop. He struggled to remember all the different causes for wrist drop. It was bilateral, too. All the traumatic causes produced a problem just on one side. It had to be a more generalized neuropathy, but one that emphasized the radial nerves and the hands. Lead poisoning, of course, could do that. Lead ... *led* ... *lead*? Was that the joke that amused Jenkins? *Lead by the hand.*

Chronic lead poisoning was common in all of Britain's heavy industrial cities. Colic, anemia, psychosis and seizures could all occur, but wrist drop was one of the most typical features. There was a way to make the diagnosis for sure.

Oddly enough, it was Doyle who'd told Wally much of what he knew about lead poisoning. He was writing a story about a lead pipe worker who killed a man in a murderous frenzy but escaped hanging because of some sure sign that he suffered from lead poisoning. But what on earth was the sign? Wally couldn't remember.

Jenkins seemed to be reading his mind and might have even given Wally a subtle wink. The man rubbed his tongue across his teeth and winked again, this time more emphatically.

McLeish was looking out the window, affecting boredom with repeated sighs and drumming his fingers on the window sill.

Wally now remembered what the diagnostic sign was. In cases of chronic lead poisoning a blue-black line almost invariably formed at the margin of the gums. In Arthur's story the murderer had been asked to show the line to the judge.

"Could you open your mouth, please, Mister Jenkins?"

The man acquiesced, with a look of relief, as if he'd been praying for Wally to solve the riddle. A heavy dark line was stenciled around the base of every tooth.

At that moment, the examining room door burst open and in strode William Macewen, his shoulders pinned back and chin thrust forward.

"Morning, Archie. How's Wally doing?"

McLeish looked flustered, like a naughty boy caught stealing.

"Not very well, I'm afraid. Seems your man McConnochie doesn't have a clue what's going on."

"Oh, I very much doubt that, my friend."

"Don't know what you see in him." This last comment was spoken in a hushed voice, but still loud enough for Wally to hear.

"Excuse me, sir," Wally interrupted, pretending not to notice what was going on between his two teachers.

"Yes?" It was McLeish who answered.

"Should I be looking for more than one diagnosis?"

"One would be more than enough," said McLeish. "As long as it were the right one," he added, with a sarcastic laugh. He turned to Macewen and raised his eyebrows as if to prove his point. "But we haven't got all day."

Still looking at the patient, Wally said, "I believe Mister Jenkins has plumbism, chronic lead poisoning, complicated by a severe form of neuritis. I can't be sure how he came by it, but if he had worked at the Clydebank Lead Pipe factory, for example, he might—"

"Jolly good show, Wally." Macewen was smiling from ear to ear. "Satisfied?" he said to McLeish.

McLeish glared back at both of them then turned to speak to the patient. "That'll be all for today, Mister Jenkins."

"E did well, dint he, sir? Got it first pop, dint he? E's a proper smart one. Even told you where I worked."

"Yes, yes, now off you go, Jenkins."

"Come on, Wally. You deserve a pint," said Macewen. "Archie stuck you with a stinker of a case, but you figured it out anyway. He's used that case a few times before and I believe everyone else has failed."

Wally vowed to buy Doyle a bottle of whisky next time they met. If it hadn't been for his detective stories, he'd have failed, too. Not a doubt about it.

12 Tripping Around

Once the long-winded speeches and the formal handshakes of the graduation ceremony were over, Wally headed out of Glasgow to visit his friends. That same day, the sun emerged from behind six months of cloud.

Over in Edinburgh, Doyle had just graduated, too, and it was him that Wally visited first.

His friend had gained in girth and in garrulousness. Arthur's time aboard the *Bristol* had been fantastic, even if only half his stories were true. Whatever were his skills as a ship's surgeon, there was no doubting his abilities as a raconteur. When he talked about the whore houses of Port Elizabeth or the Arab bazaars in Zanzibar, he could paint a picture so vivid that the listener might very well be there with him.

"But enough of silly nostalgia, Wally." said Doyle, eventually. "Where are you going to practice? Have you decided to stay in your adopted Scotland or are you taking yourself back to the glorious land of your birth?"

"I'm not sure," said Wally.

"Not a true contest. Scotland's really your best choice. The very *dunt*, I say."

"Yes, it's been very kind to me, I agree. But I'm not sure I want to settle down yet."

"Settle down? Nobody's talking about settling down. It's a medical license they gave you, not a marriage license."

"I don't mean that," said Wally, his brown complexion hiding a flush.

"Well, man, what do you mean?"

"I want to see more of the world, Arthur. You yourself have been places I've not been—Africa, Greenland, all kinds of places."

"You'll have time for that later, once you've built up your practice. I'm going to try my hand in the town of Bristol. If that doesn't pan out, I might go and join my good friend, George Budd, in Liverpool. You could come with me either place. Think of the fun we'd have. The stories we'd invent would keep us going on the slower days and the money would make up for the effort of working on the harder ones."

"Thanks, Arthur. And I might be back begging for your help in next to no time. But I feel the need to travel more, to escape the cities and to see new things. I want to taste the unexpected."

"Say no more. Say no more. I had a suspicion that you'd probably want to go back to sea. You're always at your happiest when you're talking about the *Bristol*, leaky old tub that she is. Poxy would have you back in a flash, that's for sure."

"I hope so."

Arthur gave a little chuckle and thumped his fist on the table.

"Wally, I have to believe that I'm not the only person you're going to visit on this trip."

"Oh, why do you say that?"

"Your lady friend up in Dundee—the one who's related to old Poxy. What's her name again?"

"Helen."

"Yeah, now be honest with me. You're going to stop up there and see that wee lassie, aren't you?"

"You're a sly old dog. There's no hiding any damned thing from you. Yes, that's where I'm headed next."

"Well, mind how you go, my friend. Her intentions and yours may not be quite the same."

Wally had been worried about that very thing. When he wrote to Helen announcing his intention of visiting, her enthusiastic reply left no doubt in his mind that she thought he was chasing her, not chasing another job at sea. Had she known Wally's mind, she likely wouldn't have been so inviting and wouldn't have declared so openly that her uncle, Captain Percival Pockletree, would be ensconced there that very week.

"And, Wally, you'll have to stop running away from your childhood one day!"

This last comment of Arthur's haunted Wally as he journeyed by train up to Dundee. Was that what he was doing, running away from himself? He twisted and turned all the options around in his mind, without getting anywhere other than to convince himself that this was not the time to be deepening his relationship with Helen or any other lass. The view outside the train window rumbled past, whetting Wally's appetite for more travel.

Helen's house was up the coast, a couple of miles north of Dundee, on the road to Monifeith. Wally walked, rather than take a hansom cab ride, so saving himself sixpence but gaining muddy boots and dirt splashed on his clothes in the process.

"Here, look at you," said Helen, when she opened the front door. "You're all covered in grime. Take your boots off—and your jacket, too."

"I'm sorry," said Wally. "I would've taken a cab if I'd …"

"Now, shush! I'll not hear another word about it. I'm not the kind of woman to be afraid of a few specks of dirt."

Wally peered down the hallway. He could see an umbrella stand, a hat rack and an assortment of boots and slippers. Spying a black peaked cap, he said, "Is your uncle here already?"

"Yes, he got in yesterday. He's in the kitchen having a cuppa tea."

"I should pay my respects to him, then."

"Wouldn't you like to see Walter first?"

"Walter?"

"My wee lad. He's two years old now, you know."

"Oh, of course." Wally paused to concoct an excuse for forgetting all about her little one. "I thought he might've been asleep. I wouldn't want to wake him."

The tiny stone cottage was cold and damp, the furnishings old and dark. This is summer, thought Wally. Imagine what it must be like in all those six months of winter.

After much nonsensical chat with the youngster, Wally was finally released to go visit Poxy in the kitchen. The old salt was sitting in a wicker chair, reading a newspaper. He looked up as Wally came in.

"Wally, how nice to see you."

"Nice to see you, too, sir."

The two men shook hands in a formal Scottish way and Poxy motioned for Wally to sit.

"Helen tells me you're a full doctor now."

"As of a week ago."

"And you've come straight up here to see her, I take it?" His lisp made it sound as if he'd said *stwait*.

"Well, yes and no ... sir."

"Meaning?"

"Well, I did rather hope to see you, sir."

"Oh, and why would that be? Not in trouble, I hope. Are you?"

"No, I was hoping you might know of a ship I could join. The *Bristol* would be nice, but another ship would be satisfactory, too ... if you recommended me to it."

"Well, the *Bristol* is having a refit. She'll be in dry dock for the next three months. But let me check with Leadenhall Street. They might very well have something."

"What did I miss?" Helen said, as she entered the kitchen, baby Walter on her arm.

"Seems Wally wants to go back to sea, my girl."

Helen's face paled, and she turned her attention to the coal scuttle. "I see we're nearly out of coal. Keep an ear open for little Walter while I go and get some."

"I think you've surprised her," said Poxy.

"Maybe she'd been expecting me—"

"The less said the better."

And so with the atmosphere in the house quite chilly, Wally decided to pack up and leave for Glasgow the following morning. He remained on cordial terms with Helen, but the spark in her manner had clearly been extinguished. He might as well have thrown cold water in her face. He wanted to say sorry but he heeded Poxy's admonition and said nothing. After all, what could he say? He couldn't adequately explain his decision even to himself—certainly not in any logical way. The openness of the sea, the excitement of a fresh port, meeting new and different people—what logic would those reasons have for a sensible mother like Helen, a kind and homely girl who sought the best for her little child and wanted a secure and happy future with a settled husband.

"I'll write you at your digs," said Poxy. "I expect Helen's got the address." The old seafarer seemed to understand all right.

"She does. And I hope you'll write me, too," said Wally, looking at Helen.

"Yes, I'm sure I'll find the time," said Helen.

But Wally wasn't sure she would.

13   Tropical Ills

A letter from Poxy arrived a long two weeks later. It was brief and to the point. A barque, the *Arabella*, under Captain Hollister Trumble, was due to sail for Jamaica in a month's time. She would leave from Liverpool and would be carrying a cargo of cloth and machine parts. Her crew numbered about thirty and they would need a doctor, someone who was capable of dealing with tropical diseases, as there had been an outbreak of fever on board on her last trip. Was Wally game to make the voyage? If so, he should send a letter of acceptance post haste.

Wally was delighted. Here was a chance to exchange cold and gloomy Scotland for the hot and sunny Caribbean. As a bonus, he'd meet Africans who'd been roughly transplanted, as slaves, and he'd learn about their native culture. Maybe it would be like going home to New Zealand, but even better because he would be watching free and solo from the outside, not being peered at as an indigenous biracial oddity as he was in his homeland.

But did he know enough about tropical diseases? That area was maybe his weakest. Surgery was his forte, and tropical diseases had clearly not been much of a priority at medical school in frosty Glasgow.

He shared his concern with Dr Macewen.

"Wally, as you know, I'm not familiar with that field but my friend, Pat Manson, most certainly is. He's been away in Formosa and has come up with all kinds of new ideas. Elephantiasis is his biggest interest—excuse the pun—but I bet he's a master of all those wog diseases."

"Thank you, sir. But if he's in China—"

"No, that's the thing. He's back in Aberdeenshire now, having a bit of a rest. He went to medical school there, and that's his home when he's not gallivanting around the world.

"I must meet him, then."

"You shall. But be prepared. He's an unusual man: part scientist, part evangelist. He has a fixation on worms getting into our bodies. Even as a kid, he was fascinated by worms—once shot a neighbor's cat and surgically removed a tapeworm from its gut."

The train ride to Aberdeen took less than six hours, but the twenty five miles inland to Manson's grey stone mansion, Littlewood, nestled close to the Grampian Mountains, took most of the next day, what with renting and watering a horse and periodically stopping for directions at isolated brae-side crofters' cottages.

Wally carried with him a letter of introduction from Macewen and a large blank notebook—he knew of no textbook that would help.

Doctor Manson was sitting on his doorstep, peeling off long fishing waders, when Wally arrived. He read Macewen's letter and laughed, "Well, how is the old so-and-so? It's been years since I've laid eyes on him."

"He's a great surgeon, sir, and highly respected in many countries."

"I'm not surprised."

Manson had a kind face, one molded by seeing life at its most intense. He was probably no more than forty years old but already his hair was mostly gray and his shoulders drooped with exhaustion. He looked like a Scottish nobleman who'd just returned from a long and bitter campaign.

"And what is it you'd like to know, Wally?" he said, placing Macewen's letter down next to his angling rod and fishing basket.

"Well, I know very little about tropical illnesses and if I'm to be of any use on board the *Arabella*, I'll need to know a lot more. I may have to deal with folk from Jamaica, Cuba and the Bahamas, and Lord-knows where else. There's bound to be yellow fever and dengue and malaria, all kinds of things I've scarcely heard of."

"I'm not sure I can help you all that much, my friend. My short spells at sea are mostly taken up with writing and, yes, sometimes playing bridge. What's more, I'm a worm man myself and whatever causes yellow jack and malaria it's sure as hell not a worm. But I do have a theory and perhaps we can learn some things together."

"I don't see how I can teach you anything, sir."

"Look at it this way. You're going to be in the hotbed of that damned problem. Perhaps we can try out some new approaches." The more Manson talked, the more he seemed to shed his lethargy.

"Experiments, you mean?"

"Yes."

"With the sailors as guinea pigs?"

"In a way, but I wouldn't call them that. Let's think of them as co-conspirators."

"Together in a greater cause."

"Och aye!" Manson clapped Wally on the back. His face was beaming. A new adventure had begun. "Come, let's find Polly. She'll show you to your room." Polly was the housekeeper and general factotum. She ministered to all three Mansons, Patrick and his elderly parents; she cooked, cleaned, washed and ironed in a never-ending parade of chores, never once showing a smile and rarely uttering a word. She'd been with the family since Patrick was a boy and she lived in a room near the back of the house. She was easily summoned by the pull of a bell cord.

For two weeks, Wally and Manson talked. They quickly became friends, casting for trout together on the Don, shooting grouse on the moors and drinking malt whisky in front of a log fire in Little-wood's grand oak-paneled sitting room at night. Occasionally Manson's parents would sit awhile with them after dinner but all the talk of medical matters would soon drive them off to bed.

Despite Manson's declaration that he had little experience of medicine in the hot sticky parts of the world, he proved to be an encyclopedia of new knowledge for Wally and he outlined some of the miracles that medical science and public health had wrought.

Scurvy, once the dreaded Captain of Death at sea, had been abolished by James Lind—another Scot, Manson reminded Wally—and a daily drink of one ounce of lemon juice. Vaccination was introduced into the Navy around 1800, so the scourge of smallpox was rarely a problem. Similarly, typhus had been dramatically reduced by vigorous programs of de-lousing, personal hygiene and rat extermination. Boiling the drinking water had gotten rid of typhoid.

Unfortunately, what was left was a wide and morbid spectrum of virulent fevers. They went by a slew of different names:

intermittent and undulant, relapsing and remittent, quarantine and non-quarantine, and miasmic.

Bad air, *mal aria*, was blamed for most of them, hence the term *malaria*. The putrid air around a low marsh or that arising from rotting vegetation was especially suspect. Cases of malaria were most frequent amongst watering parties who slept overnight on land while filling the ship's water casks. Rotting timbers on a ship were thought to harbor malaria as well, leading to the liberal dousing of the ship with carbolic.

Unfortunately, none of these measures had damped down the spread of the most fulminant and deadly fever of all—yellow fever. So great was the fear it instilled in the hearts of sailors that they took to calling a fever anything but that. They might talk of bilious or Barbados fever, American plague or Dutch fever, anything to avoid acknowledging the dreaded yellow fever.

"That's the real enemy now, Wally, at least in the Caribbean, that damnable sea of fever."

"What's it like? How does it show itself?"

"This is all hearsay, mind you."

"I understand," said Wally, his pen and notebook standing ready. "I need whatever you can tell me."

They were sitting on a wooden bench that overlooked the leafy vegetable garden. The golden sun was low in the sky and a herd of cows gathered near the barn for milking. Sickness and the sea seemed a long way away.

"You and I both know tuberculosis for what it is, right?"

"I know it to be a mean and methodical killer," said Wally. He thought of his old doctor friend, Chisholm, and how he'd suffered, rotting away from the inside out.

"Well, yellow fever is just as bad, but it does its dirty work in a week. No subtlety, no time for goodbyes, not a moment for self-pity. You get it one day, you're delirious the next and maybe dead on the third."

"Does everyone die?"

"No, but most do. Curiously, the few who survive never succumb to yellow fever again. They're resistant to it. Bit like the poor Christians who were thrown to the lions. If you weren't mauled and eaten, you were given your freedom."

"The ship as a coliseum."

"Aye."

"But the first signs, are they mostly those of fever?"

"I've heard it said that a blinding headache is the first clue a man will get, then the fever starts. It may very well remit after the first day and the poor fool thinks he's better. But then it boomerangs back. He shivers and shakes and takes on the rigors, all within the space of another few hours. The mind goes quickly, Wally, and the crazed victim thrashes about at any brave soul who would try to minister to him. Then he'll vomit—a black and putrid efflux that smells of the devil—and soon he's gone, as dead as the trout we pulled from the Don yesterday, and just as quick."

"It makes me sick just to hear about it," said Wally.

"And you know the funny thing?"

"None of it sounds funny."

"The man who dies from yellow fever—he's often never yellow."

"Oh, then why's it called yellow fever?"

"You have to live for at least a few days for the yellow jaundice to show. It's also the color of the flag a stricken ship will fly when approaching port—the quarantine flag—the dreaded yellow jack."

Wally wondered how he would cope with such a sinister opponent on the high seas. What steps would he take to protect the men? Would he himself become infected?

"There must be something that can work—to help, I mean."

Manson shrugged his shoulders. "Oh, there will be, but it's nothing that's been tried so far."

"You sound so pessimistic, but you said you have a theory."

"And I do! But before I tell you, remember I've never seen a case. We just don't get it in Asia."

"That's no matter. I've not seen one either, though I fear I will before too long."

"Well, a man by the name of Findlay—a Scotsman, too, by God—presented an astonishing paper in Washington a few months ago. He has evidence that links yellow fever with the humble mosquito. The devilish little blighter could carry the organism that causes the disease, injecting it into the hapless victim when it bites."

"And you think we might be able to beat it if we banish mosquitoes from the ship?"

"It's worth a try, Wally. But it'll be up to you to figure out how to do that. It won't be easy."

14 Wally Boards the Arabella

Every captain has a nickname. Few of these monikers are complimentary and most identify the man's most malignant foible with piercing accuracy. It was no accident that Hollister Trumble was known throughout the merchant marine as Captain Bumble. Ships in his command had run aground, taken on water, nurtured epidemics and harbored more than one mutiny. Yet, for all that, Bumble was generally liked—he was not a harsh or vindictive man and his long list of disasters were, in part, bad luck, engendering more compassion than resentment by his men and those who hired him.

Trumble was up on the quarterdeck when Wally first boarded the *Arabella*. He was unmistakably the captain, in his neatly pressed shirt, striped jacket and peaked cap. He was leaning against the taffrail, making notes on a large sheet of paper, probably the ship's manifest. The day was unusual for Liverpool, with clear skies and little wind.

"Mornin', sir," said Wally.

"Yes?" answered Trumble, absentmindedly.

"Doctor McConnochie. Reporting for duty."

"Oh, good! Good! I've been so looking forward to meeting you."

"And me you, sir."

"Percival tells me good things about you." It was odd to hear Pockletree's formal first name. "Let me show you your quarters. There'll be plenty of time later to talk about your duties."

The *Arabella* was smaller than the ship Wally sailed in to London, the *Bristol*, and he was not surprised that his cabin also served as the dispensary. The crowded space was cluttered with leftovers from the last occupant, an untidy man with a fondness for liquor, judging by the pile of gin bottles that filled a gunny sack lying open on the bunk. A heavy smell of stale tobacco exposed another of his habits.

"You know I'll have to rummage through things and come up with a list of what's needed for the voyage," said Wally.

The captain nodded. "Of course. We're pretty much out of medicines—I know that. You heard what happened?"

"No. Captain Pockletree just said that you had an outbreak of fever."

"Well, we started with a full complement of men, twenty-five, and ended up with ten. The doctor was one of the first to go and Billy Scaggs soon followed him over the gunwale. Billy had been my first mate for ten years on many a different ship. He was worth ten men, just himself. The carpenter and the sailmaker and nearly all the able seamen died, just in the space of a week. It was hell." Trumble was trembling and he had tears in his eyes.

"How on earth did you manage?"

"I near as ever ..."

"A skeleton crew."

"Just one more voyage—that's all I'm going to put up with." Trumble was biting his lower lip and climbing up the companionway. He seemed to be in a private world, deaf to anything Wally was saying. It was to be an image that Wally would come to know very well.

The remnants of the old crew were on shore leave and the new recruits hadn't yet arrived, assuming, of course, that men could be found to volunteer on a ship with such a history of fever and death and with a master known to all as Captain Bumble. It was a good time for Wally to have a snoop around.

The bulk of the ship, below decks, comprised a large hold for the cargo. Heavy stanchions created a number of compartments to keep the cargo from moving about in rough seas and the lines that were used to secure bolts of linen dangled from the beams. In a few places the woodwork seemed soggy with moisture and makeshift bolsters had been crudely fitted as temporary supports for who knows how long.

The hatch leading to the bilges was open but in the dim light Wally couldn't make out what mysteries lay beneath. There would surely be rats scuttling around down there, and cockroaches too, but bilge water would surely be kept to a minimum even if only to protect the cargo of linen.

The foc's'le needed a good cleaning out. Decayed food scraps, dirty clothes and musty bedding were a breeding ground for maggots, lice and bugs, and a likely place for incubating fevers. Wally hoped this was a result of the *Arabella* being short-handed and not a sign of slovenliness on Trumble's part. But, of course, he couldn't be sure.

The superstructure of a ship was mostly a mystery to Wally. He counted three masts: the first two bearing square sails which were untidily furled up and the third, towards the stern, rigged fore and aft. Even he could see that the jumble of lines and shrouds that made up the rigging would need considerable attention before the ship set sail. Coils of new line lay heaped ready for that task.

In the galley, amidships, he was surprised to find someone else, a black man chipping soot from the innards of the stove. The man was just as startled to see Wally.

"Hey, man, what you doin' here?"

"I'm the new doctor—Wally—Wally McConnochie."

"Oh, you are, are you? Master must be mighty pleased to have you. Answer to his prayers, you are."

"I don't know if I'm that important, especially as—"

"You de answer. Take my word for it. We don't get any men to sail the ship if we don't have a doctor. Don't tell me you don't know the problems we been having."

The man's firm declaration didn't make Wally feel any more secure about the *Arabella* or his role in managing its medical affairs.

"What's you name, sir?" Wally asked.

"Charles Spencer, but you can call me Charlie. Everyone else does, except my parents—they still prefer to call me Spencer."

"Where do you hail from, Charlie."

"I'm from Port Royal—yunno, Jamaica—land of coffee and coconuts."

"Are we going there on this trip?"

"If not there, heaven or the other place. You been there?"

"What?"

"Where you from?"

"I'm from New Zealand."

"I heard of that. They got colored people there. Like you, perhaps."

"Yes, I'm part Maori. My mother was—is—Maori."

"Is that why the Master hired you?"

"What do mean?"

"The yellow jack don't strike us colored folk—least that's what the Master thinks."

"Really?"

"They even call it the stranger's disease. But I seen it kill many black folk in Port Royal. It's just that white people, like the Master, don't take any notice, us being less important and all."

Wally wished that Bumble had been right. What a turnaround if his skin color could, for once, work to his advantage. But more likely he would be asked to expose himself to even higher risks because he was thought to be immune. In Glasgow he'd been vaccinated against smallpox, knowing a doctor would be likely to have to face it somewhere—the scar was clearly visible on his upper arm, identifying him as someone protected. His Maori color was another mark, but one whose meaning was false. His shield against yellow fever existed only in the minds of ignorant Englishmen.

"Are you the cook, Charlie?" asked Wally.

"Lord no, I ain't that important. I'm the mess hand, but I can do a turn at the stove. Mister Blodgett likes me to help, if he's at all under the weather." Wally had heard that turn of phrase before, usually referring to a man who was regularly tipsy or a flat-out drunk.

"The sozzler's mate, then?"

"Now don't you go saying that. Mister Blodgett's no sozzler, though he does like a nip now and again. Anyway, he takes care of me, good and all."

"You're lucky both of you escaped the fever."

"We sleep up here in the galley most nights, away from all those germs in the foc's'le. Mister Blodgett thinks that's what saved us."

And maybe away from all the mosquitoes, thought Wally. Maybe the cook, sozzled or not, was onto something.

15 Preparing to Depart

The Port of Liverpool was cluttered with ships, large and small, steam and sail, paddleboats, barges, clippers and smacks, all intent on loading or unloading, provisioning and repairs. Steam-driven cranes hoisted up bulky cargos of carpet and paper and stevedores worked block-and-tackles to lug aboard food stores, sail cloth, kit bags and livestock. The loud clattering of chains, the shunting of locomotives and an occasional fog horn blast interrupted the constant dockside buzz of multilingual shouts, commands and insults.

The *Arabella* was not the shabbiest of the couple of dozen barques in the harbor, but she was far from the smartest. Patches of new paint did little to disguise makeshift repairs, and ubiquitous lashings of tar only emphasized the wide cracks that had opened up along the bulwarks. She was not fit for anything more than easy passages back and forth to the Caribbean, riding the trade winds on the way over and the Gulf Current coming back.

Wally smiled as words of his mother flashed into his mind. *Manawa te taonga o te pa!* Behold the treasure of the village! How she had often said that when confronted by a disappointingly small gift or an especially objectionable person. She wouldn't have approved of his sailing down the Otago harbor in so derelict a ship, let alone cross the Atlantic Ocean. But she wasn't here; she was on the other side of the world, and soon to be reading letters about the handsome clipper he was embarking upon. A lie, to be sure, but better that than she worry unnecessarily. He'd be safe in Jamaica by the time she read his words.

And what had become of Kotuku, his soul-mate from Otakau? He'd not given much thought to her in recent months. The prospects he most yearned for were those of a free-spirit life on the open sea and the sense of adventure in finding new friends and places to explore: no burden of compromise between brown skin and white and no tethering of his emotions to one person or place. He was in love with whatever was new—the old was history and best put away on the shelf. And he still was young, and he had the dreams that yearlings had before they were old enough to race.

The new first mate was called Tosh Mitford, a short, almost dwarfish, muscular man in his fifties who had spent his younger days as a circus performer. His skill walking the high-wire made him a natural for scampering up the rigging and, afraid of nothing and nobody, he was more than a match for any seaman who wanted a fight. He once bit off someone's thumb and he could immobilize a man with a punch to the solar plexus or a kick in the groin.

"Once we sail, you and me can play cards," he said to Wally, taking no notice of the standing order that forbade gambling on the *Arabella*.

"I don't know if we should," said Wally.

"Of course we can. I enforce the rules around here—but only the rules I want to enforce. You understand, don't you?"

Wally was beginning to.

"And you and me'll get along fine, as long as you keep me posted on any little goings-on around the ship."

"Such as?"

"Well, such as if you hear any grumbling about yours-truly or any schemes to create mischief or cause an injury to befall him. Keep a special eye on our honorable wogs—the Indian gentleman, whom I most properly call a lascar, and our two Tartar guests. I call 'em that because I doubt they expect to expend more than one ounce of sweat aboard this ship. Mind you, sir, they have yet to hear from me."

There was a touch of legalese in the way that Tosh spoke and Wally later discovered that Tosh's father had been a prominent lawyer in the City of London, rejecting his son when his stunted growth became apparent and sending him off to boarding school at the age of twelve. There, Tosh was taunted and ridiculed and he ran away, at first living off the street, but then, falling on his feet as it were, he joined the circus as a high diver, a skill he'd learned by diving from the London Bridge into the River Thames at a penny a time. The passers-by he entertained came to know him as "The Flying Dolphin."

The showman in Tosh appealed to Wally. His own gambling persona, King Tawhai, could have played alongside "The Flying Dolphin" on any bridge or in any circus in London. The two of them had much else in common, too: a curiously distinctive appearance, a set of special skills and a sense of being alone on life's voyage. All of these characteristics were present in those who sailed the open seas, but it took unusual common sense to adapt to them with good humor and turn them to useful advantage.

"Have you ever been on a ship afflicted with yellow fever?" said Wally.

"Bilious fever? Aye, and I never want to see or smell it again."

"Men died, did they?"

"Yes, and not all as you might think."

"Well, I don't know much about any shipboard fevers. Tell me more!"

"The worst nightmare we had on the *Anglais* was what befell the bosun's mate. The incident occurred right in the middle of a bilious fever scourge aboard the ship. At eight a.m. of the morning in question he complained of his head, and by ten he was in the sick room grinding his teeth in delirium. Minutes later he appeared on deck, stark naked and brandishing the cook's axe. He was a giant of an Irishman to start with, so the sight of him rushing madly about the deck caused terror in all who set eyes on him."

"I can imagine," said Wally.

"He struck out at everything in his way, while the foam flew from his gaping mouth. When he came upon the steersman, he lunged at him with his axe, so frightening the poor man that he scampered up the rigging in fear for his life. The wheel was now unattended and it spun free, putting the ship into a series of wild pitches and yaws. Our rampaging madman was caught unawares by these violent movements and he tumbled headlong off the after-deck, his chest impaling onto the upturned edge of the axe."

"Did he survive?"

"He died right there and then, in a sea of blood like a butchered seal. If he hadn't been such a habitual drunk, I might've felt sorry for him."

"Good grief, what a terror!"

"It certainly was, while it lasted. But for all that, no-one else was injured by the maniac, and we shrugged it off as a bit of comic relief, a distraction from the wearisome burden of caring for the feverish and disposing of our dead compatriots, us all being of pure British blood aboard the *Anglais*. Not that I have anything to say against yourself, my honorable friend."

"Nor did I suspect it, sir."

Wally hadn't yet talked with Trumble about Manson's theory of mosquitoes being a carrier for yellow fever, but he thought that Tosh might be a good sounding board.

"I assume you were in the Caribbean when this all happened."

"We most certainly were—just come out of Cuba. No more than a couple of days from Havana, as I remember."

"And had the mosquitoes been bad that trip."

"They're always a problem down there—big as horse flies and bite like piranhas. Can't rightly recall 'em being especially bad on that trip. Why? What's that got to do with anything?"

"A friend of mine thinks they may have something to do with the spread of yellow fever."

"Poppycock! Even I know that can't be right."

"Why?"

"Well, we have mosquitoes aboard the ship—any ship—all the time, every trip. But the fever only hits every now'n again, with no rhyme or reason."

Wally could see that Tosh had a point and even if Doctor Manson's theory was right, it would be hard to convince Trumble and the crew. He was the inexperienced one and he was not likely to be listened to if the facts seemed contradictory.

"The worst thing aboard a ship is rum," said Tosh. "It wrecks more havoc than any innocent mosquito could."

The lockers in Wally's cabin-come-dispensary were in bad need of repair and Captain Trumble promised help from the carpenter just as soon as the ship got underway. Of course that meant temporarily storing all the medical supplies loose around the cabin, some heaped in boxes and the rest in sacks. Bottles of vitriol and oil had to be packed in an upright position to avoid spillage and jars of alum and lemon salts tightly corked. It was less of a disadvantage that so many containers were empty.

Wally made a list of what needed to be requisitioned prior to sail. Quinine and laudanum, ether, opium pills, tincture of iodine and Glauber salts were essential. Sufficient castor oil, Epsom salts and smelling salts were already in stock, but he needed more adhesive plasters, bandages and mercury.

His training was strongest in surgery, yet it was medicaments and pharmaceuticals he'd most likely need. Lancets, forceps, needles and silk might come in handy for a laceration but they had no power against a fever, at least not a stealthy destroyer like yellow fever never showing an abscess or pus pocket as a target for the knife. A trepan might relieve the pressure of a brain hemorrhage or a tumor but it was useless in dealing with a toxic delirium. He was to be tested in a game with no known rules using tools that wouldn't work.

16 The Carpenter

The *Arabella* cast off on a cold, misty morning, with little wind. A little coal-powered tugboat guided her through the crowded harbor and released her into the unusually placid Irish Sea. The pilot waved goodbye and Captain Trumble ordered the sails fully set to make the most of the meager breeze.

"All ready for'ard?" he called to Tosh.

"Aye, aye, sir!"

"Let go'n'haul."

"Tops'l yard, a pull," called Tosh to the sailors in the yards above him.

Wind filled the sails and the ship jerked forward.

"Helm's a-lee"

"Helm's a-lee, sir."

The new crew members had their first chance to measure up their fellow sailors and to figure out who on their watch were shirkers and loafers. On any ship, sailors had ways to encourage such people to conform, by ragging, bullying or beating, these diversions creating much of the sport in the early days out from port.

Tosh was their immediate commander. He assigned the watch duties and supervised the care of the rigging and made sure that enough braided cordage—he called it *sennit*—was readily available for emergency repairs in times of foul weather. However, amongst such a raw rabble, other informal hierarchies soon formed, led by the men who were the toughest, the meanest or the most fearless.

Samuel Edwards was hard-working but his gentle demeanor and fastidiousness made him a natural target for harassment. As ship's carpenter, he worked the day alone, but at night in the foc's'le, tidying his kit or sketching shapes in charcoal on brown wrapping paper, he'd hear the uncouth jeers of his tormentors. He would answer these crudities with a smile of resignation, never deigning to counter them directly.

Wally talked with Edwards as he fashioned new cabinets and lockers for the surgeon's cabin.

"Matlock. It's in Derbyshire," Edward's said, when Wally asked him where he hailed from.

"Never been there myself," said Wally.

"Not many folks has. It's a bit remote, but maybe more beautiful for that." His accent intrigued Wally—it was more lilting than the accents he'd heard in London, softer and rounder, more like a Welshman's.

"You never heard of the Derwent?" Edwards added.

"No."

"Well, it's a big river—at least, I used think it so. Big for them parts."

"Why did you leave?"

"No work. No good paying jobs, anyway. We had a big paper mill but new jobs there were few and far between. I wanted to be a painter, an artist like, but you need special training for that and my family ... well, we didn't have much money, did we?"

"So you went to sea."

"No, not at first. I started an apprenticeship, to become a carpenter, but I ran into a spot of bother."

"Oh?"

"I'd prefer not to talk about it."

"That's all right," said Wally, shrugging his shoulders. "We all have our secrets."

Wally thought about the dark secret he had carried with him onto the *Bristol* when he left New Zealand. Many years before, his father, Jock McConnochie, had shot and killed a beast of a man, a whaler by the name of Grigor Clucas. He did it to save the life of a Maori princess whom Clucas had raped and meant to kill before selling her head on the macabre London market that valued tattoos above all else. In fairy-tale fashion, Jock married the princess and they named their second child Walter, though most called him Wally.

The tragedy of Clucas's death haunted the McConnochies for ever after. What should have been a source of pride for Jock—his valor in saving an innocent life—became his burden. The McConnochie family was largely ostracized in the Scottish settlement of Dunedin, not for their mixed-race marriage as one might have

92

expected, but for Jock's breaking an unspoken code by punishing one of his own.

On joining the *Bristol*, Wally was shocked to find that the first mate was the son of the man his father had shot and he spent much of the voyage trying to hide the truth about his past. But eventually the secret was exposed, as secrets usually are. In retrospect, Wally was pleased that it was. It lay to rest a nightmare from his past.

He pretended not to be intrigued as to what secret Samuel Edwards was hiding, but in truth he was eager to know. Not that he had any wish to pry, nor did he want any hold over Edwards but he felt that secrets and subterfuge were powerful illuminations, revealing more about a person than scrutiny of his façade ever could.

His old friend and mentor in the New Zealand goldfields, Doc Chisholm, had a saying: a man's true character is reflected in the mirror of his secrets. And we see ourselves and others a little clearer when we look into that mirror.

The *Arabella* slogged her way down the choppy Bay of Biscay and on towards Tenerife. Even favored with a following wind, she was sluggish, moaning on the crests and shuddering in every trough, progressing at the pace of an arthritic mule. She sprang a leak in her wormy hawse timbers which the men battled to seal with tar and oakum.

"Like the old girl's unraveling," said Tosh. "Comin' apart at the seams." But his words were no more than a sailor's grouse and he laughed at Wally's look of concern. "We'll be fine, Doc, so long as we miss the cyclones."

Trumble's plan, the one he always tried to follow, was to put in at Tenerife, in the Canary Islands, for water and fresh meat and vegetables. The people there spoke only in Spanish and showed so little hospitality that sailors aboard the *Arabella* would think twice before deserting. Crossing the North Atlantic on a rickety merchantman was more appealing than dying of starvation on an arid and inhospitable volcanic mountain in the middle of nowhere.

Trumble fussed over the sun sightings each noon. With sextant in hand and Tosh at his side he barked out readings for the first mate to record as the clock closed in on noon. In his haste he'd muddle the angles or lose sight of the horizon, requiring repeated assessments none of which could be entirely trusted. Those older salts who new old Bumble well promised his fumblings would only get worse as the seas became rougher out in the mid-Atlantic.

A cry went up amongst the crew when the lookout spotted the craggy peaks of Tenerife. The *Arabella* bobbed its way past the rocky outcrops of the southern coast and into the snug little harbor at Santa Cruz.

Once the anchor was set, Captain Trumble pointed out to Wally some of the features of the island.

"Those mountains are the Anagas. Wonderful little villages are hidden up there, some with quaint traditions and all having magnificent views of the ocean."

"Have you ever been up there, sir?"

"Well, no. We only ever stay here a day or two—unless the weather breaks, and then it'd be too dangerous to traverse the narrow mountain trails, even on a donkey."

Trumble didn't look like a hiker, with his pot-belly and bandy legs, and Wally doubted that the Old Man would challenge those hills under any circumstance.

"But the village itself must have some attractions," he asked.

"It does, but they are pretty limited."

"Where would you suggest I go?"

"The Plaza de la Candelaria has an old Castle. That's worth seeing. And I like to go to San Andres to eat the fish and local cheese. The beef is good, as well."

"Well, that's where I'll go then. I s'pose they have good fruit to eat."

"Yes, bananas and tomatoes. We'll be taking some on board. Potatoes, too, we'll pick up. But, Doctor … be careful!" Trumble wagged his fore-finger at Wally.

"Of what?"

"The people. You might confuse them, what with your brown color and your English way of speaking. Nelson hammered this town pretty badly, almost leveled it with cannon fire."

"But that must've been a hundred years ago."

"Not quite. They have long memories and they're always for revenge. They might see a dark-skinned person as a turncoat mulatto or some such thing and enjoy the chance to do you in." Trumble's frown showed he wasn't joking.

Wally thought back to the retribution his Maori ancestors took, years ago, when they massacred seventy Europeans on the *Boyd*. The ship's master—a white man, a Pakeha, had broken *tapu* when he flogged a young chief who was working aboard. Such gross disrespect merited the massacre in Maori eyes. The slain were, of course, eaten. But now, more than seventy years later, did the Pakeha still want revenge for the loss of the sailors? They very well might.

"I'll be careful," he said.

He boarded the first local tender offering to take him to the narrow wooden jetty that poked out into the harbor. The paddlers were sinewy, leather-skinned young men with rheumy eyes and their master a twisted old man smoking a pipe. They spoke no English and the master accepted Wally's shilling with an unsmiling nod.

Once his papers had been vetted by the Port Authorities, Wally set out for San Andres.

Striding along the stony track that skirted the waterfront, he was soon sweating. The sun burned on his head and with each step he kicked up dust and flies.

A little terrier joined him—white with black spots, and only three legs.

"Hello, little fella," he said.

The dog looked up, eyes bright and tail wagging.

"You live around here?"

The terrier hobbled along beside him. Wally missed the two Labradors that he'd owned in New Zealand and there were no pets on the *Arabella*, not even a cockatoo or budgie.

They came upon a tumbledown shack where three men were sitting outside on a wooden bench, spooning thick fish soup from iron bowls and breaking handfuls of bread from a large loaf they shared. A rough sign nailed on the shack read "Pescado y Marisco." Wally hoped that meant it was a place where he could eat.

"Excuse me, sir," he said to one of the men.

The man grunted and continued eating.

"Can I eat here?"

Still there was no response from any of the three men but a fat woman in a black dress pushed open a slat door and beckoned Wally inside. She pointed to a chair and a small table. The curtains were drawn and the room was dark. Wally could vaguely make out a couple of other tables positioned around the room.

He sat down. The men outside were laughing.

The woman waddled behind a curtain of colored beads and promptly emerged with two bowls similar to the ones he'd seen outside. They brimmed with fish soup. One bowl she put in front of Wally, the other she placed on the floor for the terrier.

"Hoy hace mucho calor," she said, but Wally didn't understand a word.

The soup was spiced with pepper and thick with chunks of white fish flesh. Both Wally and the dog consumed all that had been put before them.

The woman smiled at Wally and gave him a pat on the shoulder with her coarse hand. She puckered her lips and blew him a kiss. The men outside were laughing again.

The woman produced a mug of wine for Wally, which she also drank from. She pulled another chair up alongside his and sat down, wheezing softly. Wally could smell her sweat and wine-soaked breath.

He fumbled in his pocket and offered her a sixpence. She turned the silver coin over in her palm and then she handed it back to him. She let her hand rest on his thigh.

No amount of soup or wine could entice Wally to follow the intimate path where she was guiding him. He lurched to his feet and made for the door. He could hear the woman's screeches as he bolted back down the track, the terrier racing just as fast alongside him.

The last sound he heard from there was loud laughing from the three men outside.

"Why didn't you warn me," he said to the terrier, once they were out of range and catching their breath.

The little dog wagged its tail as if the whole episode had been a game.

"You should go home now," said Wally. "Off you go! Shoo!" But the dog hobbled and skipped alongside him, appearing intent to follow him wherever he planned to go.

Back at the *Arabella*, Captain Trumble initially took little interest in the terrier and told Wally he was free to keep him aboard if he wished.

"However, I want you to meet a new man I've just hired. Give him a look over. He's a bit odd and one rotten apple can spoil the others, eh?"

"In what way odd, sir?"

"Well, for one, he doesn't talk. Not a word. He can hear all right, but he's a mute—has been since birth, according to the dock master. He's from Tenerife but he makes his living by working Atlantic crossings. Damn fine man up the mast, apparently."

"I must say I'm a bit concerned, sir, about taking on a man from the tropics. You know he might be harboring yellow fever."

"Anyone could be, couldn't they? They've had it here, but not for months," Trumble snapped.

"Then maybe he's a carrier; someone who's immune, like others must be on the island."

"Dammit, McConnochie, so could that stupid dog of yours. A dog can get it too, you know."

"I know that, sir."

"So, either both join us—or neither!" Trumble waved his hand in a gesture of dismissal.

"I'll check the new man over, sir, right away."

The new man was at the bow, peering up the fore-mast. Wally shook his hand and explained that he was the ship's doctor. The man could understand English, and he nodded in a resigned sort of way, no doubt accustomed to being scrutinized very closely whenever he joined a new ship.

Wally felt his forehead and looked into his eyes. There was no fever and no sign of jaundice. He lay the man down and prodded his stomach and checked for any glandular enlargement. The man's lanky legs and arms looked strong and his joints were so mobile they might have been made of rubber.

A couple of crew members looked on as Wally poked and prodded, looking for reassurance that they would not catch anything bizarre from the newcomer.

Finding nothing he reported back to Trumble that all was well. The new man looked healthy enough.

"Good, then your dog can stay, too," the captain replied, with a hint of a smile.

That night Wally woke to the sound of a mosquito buzzing around his head, the first he'd heard aboard the *Arabella*.

17 Tosh's Misfortunes

30 August. Day 13. Noon. 27.39N, 19.38W. Wind NE, light. Bearing 220.

The *Arabella* edged her way out into the Atlantic. All ties with land would be lost for the next two weeks and the ship would be an isolated community, an oasis of life on a desert of water. The men looked at each other more closely and new things came to light with each scrutiny. Tosh quickly identified the cook as a lush and he made use of every opportunity to goad him and make him look silly. Blodgett's size, his hygiene—or rather lack of it—and his culinary skills were natural targets for Tosh's sharp tongue.

"Plenty of leftovers for you to eat tonight, Scruffy," he'd say, pointing to the food the men around the captain's table hadn't eaten.

In a loud whisper he might say, "I wish he'd let Charlie do all the cooking—at least he's sober enough to see what he's doing." He made these comments with a laugh, but calling the cook Scruffy and a drunk, to boot, was tantamount to slapping him on the face. Tosh must have known this, and he either didn't care or he was aiming to provoke Blodgett into a fight.

Blodgett never responded. He simply looked away, his gaze fogged with spirits, as he cleared away the plates. There was, of course, no way to know what such a mind was thinking.

For the first time, Wally took notice of what Samuel Edwards, the carpenter, was drawing in his charcoal sketches. The images were not of Derbyshire landscapes or peaceful exotic seascapes, as he had supposed, but rather they were of brutal savagery, eviscerations and mutilations, the victims mostly white and the perpetrators mostly black. The powerful violence that leapt from the drawings kept Wally from saying anything for fear his comments might be misconstrued, but he wondered if they had something to do with the "spot of bother" that Edwards had mentioned earlier—the one that had made him leave Matlock.

Even a cursory inspection revealed that the new man hired in Tenerife was more agile than anyone else aboard. So quickly could he scale the masts and so precariously could he dangle from the yards that the men started calling him The Monkey. He could even outpace Tosh, himself a circus acrobat and high-wire performer. During most of the day, and sometimes even at night, The Monkey would perch himself up along the fore topsail yard or on the crosstree above it. Whether it was his being a mute or simply his love of heights that kept him up there all alone, no-one knew.

One afternoon, a torrent of loud curses and abuses alerted the ship to an angry Tosh. His prize collection of scrimshaw had gone missing. Admittedly the lot consisted of only a couple of pieces, a whale-bone paper knife and a shark's tooth etching, but they had been months in the crafting and Tosh spoke of his scrimshander accomplishments with a pride comparable to Christopher Wren's for St Paul's cathedral. As first mate, he had the power to have the ship turned stern-over-bow to find his treasures and the culprit, and that is what he set about to do.

Before long, the stolen objects were located. They were hidden in a pottery jar and stashed behind a collection of pots and pans in the galley, a place where few had access but none more so than Mister Blodgett, the cook, and his offsider, Charlie Spencer. They spent nearly all their time in the galley. Immediately, Tosh descended on the two of them.

"All right, my good gentlemen, which of you is the perpetrator?" Tosh's highfalutin manner seemed out of place for a dwarfish little man addressing a fat cook and his wide-eyed black assistant in the cramped galley of a ship rolling with each swell of the sea, but his words brought them to attention.

"Nah me, Misser Mifford," said the cook, his words slurred with drink as they often were.

"Not me neither," echoed Charlie.

"Don't take me for a mug. I know it were one of you," said Tosh, his mouth set in a fierce grimace and his fists clenched. "And, by God, I'll knock the truth out of you, one way or other. I'll beat you round the head until you wish you'd never been born."

He paused for a breath, as if to reload. "I'll lay you down and kick you and I'll pour hot tar across your legs. I'll whip your ass so hard that you'll both be bleeding for a week. I'll—"

"Not so fast, Tosh!" said Captain Trumble, appearing at the galley door, and beckoning Tosh out onto the deck.

Once out of hearing range of the galley, Trumble said, "Settle down, man! Get a grip on yourself! We mustn't inflict such punishment on an innocent, and one or both might just be telling the truth, mightn't they?"

"I mean to find the offender, sir. And a sharp dose of corporal discomfort can loosen a man's lips soon enough." Tosh stamped his foot for emphasis.

"But if you injure the both of them, who'll cook our meals?" reproved the captain, with a cajoling smile.

"One of the midshipmen. Anyone can do better than Blodgett. The man's got his head in the rum cask most of the time." Yet Tosh's answer lacked conviction. If the men's meals were not acceptable, then they would curse and grouse all around the ship and might even slacken in their duties and delay the ship's arrival in the Islands.

"Well then, what do you suggest, sir? We can't let the bloody thief off free," said Tosh.

"Oh, I don't know. I just don't want any trouble."

"Trouble, sir? We got that already." He raised his eyebrows at Wally who had detached himself from the small group of onlookers and strolled over to join them.

"What do you think, Doctor?" said Trumble. "

Wally paused. No wonder the men called the captain Bumble, when he stoops to ask the surgeon how to manage discipline. His old captain on the *Bristol*, Percival Pockletree, would have sorted this out in double-quick time.

"Tell 'em that if they don't admit who did the stealing, you're going to give a lashing to one of them anyway. Just who, you haven't decided yet. And give 'em just sixty minutes to make their minds up who's it going to be. They'll sort it out quick enough."

Wally's plan worked more effectively than anyone might have guessed. In twenty minutes, Charlie Spencer offered himself up to Tosh, mumbling a confession and stating that he was prepared to receive his due, but the matter-of-factness of his manner and the resignation in his drooping shoulders smacked more of a convenient compromise than of real guilt.

Tosh looked more awkward than relieved to hear the outcome and he could do little more than give Charlie a sharp kick in the kneecap and a rabbit chop to the stomach.

"Here! Let that be a lesson to you, then," he said and walked off, looking no less perplexed than he'd been before Charlie's admission. The men who stood around observing these events could see the cook swaying at the galley door, smiling a gap-toothed smile and offering Charlie a mug maybe of broth but more likely of rum—whether he did so out of sympathy or as a reward for Charlie acting as his scapegoat, they couldn't tell.

"Well, that was a good way to flush the culprit out, wasn't it?" Wally said to Tosh, hoping to find his friend appeased.

"You reckon? Who's to know who really stole it?"

"What?"

"Blodgett and me'll have it out one day, you mark my words."

"Forget about it, Tosh. The whole thing's over now. You've got your carving back and you've had your say."

"You've a lot to learn, Wally," said Tosh, with a dismissive swipe of his hand.

Nobody would have thought any more about the incident if it hadn't been for what happened a few nights later.

18   A Bloody Scene

5 September. Day 19. Noon. 20.33N, 30.72W. Wind ENE, mild. Bearing 240.

Wally sat on his bunk, scratching out a letter he would send from Jamaica or wherever they made their first English port. His little dog, now with the name of Skipper, was nestled at his feet, chewing on a mutton bone. The letter was to Arthur, presumably now ensconced in a lucrative private practice, and Wally was finding it difficult to come up with any news that would match that kind of excitement. To write about the persistent drizzly weather and the sluggish westward advance of the ship would be to spell out boredom and, from his voyage around the coast of Africa, Arthur already knew the day-to-day duties of sailors and how life was lived aboard a ship. If only there had been a storm or two, with a lively ship pitching and rolling, the rail thrust skyward one second then dipping below the waves the next, like being on a very large, poorly-balanced see-saw that moves in both directions, men bruised and battered, flung out of their hammocks at night, and loud waves crashing down the companionway whenever the hatch was opened. But, no such luck. The *Arabella* plodded listlessly through gray mists and fog, the tolling of the ship's bell and the soft snap of a sail the only sounds to disturb the silent waters.

In desperation, Wally climbed up on deck to look for Tosh. Perhaps he could be mined for quirky reminiscences, the kind that Arthur thrived on.

"Ship ahoy!" called the lookout. Through gaps in the mist, Wally could see the hazy outlines of a ship, off to starboard less than half a league away and also heading west. She was a two-master, schooner rigged, quite unlike the usual trans-Atlantic merchantman and she flew no flag.

A ripple of excitement spread around the ship and a clutch of jacketed men hurried to the rail. One man swore she must be American but Tosh said she was more typical of the coasters that plied the Mediterranean ports and traded along the Northwest rim of Africa at places like Casablanca, Marrakech and Dakar and that she'd been on the same course as the *Arabella* for a couple of days now.

"A bloody corsair, as like as not," said Tosh. "Let's hope they're looking for larger fry." He ordered a watchful eye be kept on her and while she came no closer she also didn't tack away.

Day turned to night and Wally still struggled over his letter. One of the men had sprained an ankle when he slipped from the rigging onto the deck and another had a large furuncle on his buttock, but these minor ailments didn't carry much news value for doughty surgeons like Wally and Arthur. The growing swarms of mosquitoes aboard the ship appeared to be of interest only to Wally; Captain Trumble told him just to get used to them.

Just then, a loud shout went up from the deck above.

"Doc! Doc! Come quick!"

Wally grabbed his lantern and bounded up the steps of the starboard companionway and hurried out onto the deck. His little dog sensed the excitement and hobbled along behind him.

It was dark and raining and at first he could see no-one.

"Over here! Quick!" A man huddled down in the foredeck was waving him closer.

The scene illuminated by Wally's lantern was almost beyond his comprehension. Blood lay everywhere and in the midst of the largest pool lay Tosh, tongue lolling out, his face ghostly pale and his body motionless. If he wasn't dead, he was mighty close to it.

"Get the captain," said Wally. "And more lanterns."

He bent down to assess the situation. Tosh had a large gash in his lower neck and blood still pumped from its depths, from what must be the carotid artery. The jugular vein had probably been slashed as well.

Wally plunged the fingers of both his hands deep into the gaping wound in an effort to stem the flow of blood and yelled out for more help.

Two men pounded across the deck, one of them Edwards the carpenter, the other the helmsman. More men arrived, including

Blodgett and Charlie Spencer. Finally, Captain Trumble appeared in his nightshirt.

"What's going on here?" he said, in an unusually commanding tone, swinging his lantern as he approached.

"Tosh. It's Tosh," yelled Wally, kneeling over the prostrate body.

"What a bloody mess! An accident, what?" said the captain.

"Is he gone?" said Blodgett.

"The main thing is to get the bleeding stopped," Wally said frantically. "We've got to get him onto a table."

"What table?" said Trumble The only full-sized table was the one in his own cabin.

"There's only the one, sir," said Edwards, saving Wally the task of having to spell out the obvious.

"And you, Edwards," Wally continued, "I want you to hold pressure here—just like I'm doing. See, I've stopped the flow of blood with my fingers."

"Yes sir," said Edwards.

"What can I do?" asked Charlie Spencer.

"Just help us carry Tosh down to the captain's cabin. I'll look after his head. You others lift his arms and legs. Come on now, look lively!"

"Yes, sharp about it!" said Trumble. "You're in charge, Wally."

Altogether five of them stumbled and lurched their way down to the captain's cabin until they were able to lay little Tosh down on the bare oak table where Wally and Tosh had dined with the captain just a couple of hours before.

Tosh looked moribund other than for some irregular gurgling gasps. Wally felt for a radial pulse but wasn't sure he could feel one.

"Take your hands away—slowly," he said to Edwards.

Dark blood, some of it frothy, welled briskly into the wicked, gaping hole, suggesting that some circulation still survived, but probably very little.

"Hands back on! Hold more pressure. I'll get my instruments," said Wally.

The surgery proceeded through the night. In the flickering light of the swaying lanterns, the men took turns holding pressure above and below the sources of bleeding.

Wally spread the wound wide open with two retractors and tilted Tosh'd head back by propping his shoulders up with a roll of sailcloth. Some bleeding appeared to come from the region of the external jugular vein, but no such structure was visible and a fastidious search might compromise what little chance for survival Tosh still had. Wally made the quick decision to wrap heavy silk mattress sutures into where he guessed the external jugular might have been. It was a move that his old teacher, William Macewen, had used in similar life-and-death cases.

With vigorous swabbing, using strips of gauze, he could peer more deeply into the wound and distinguish the nearly-severed carotid artery and jugular vein, both oozing blood despite the best efforts of Edwards and his helpers. The cut ends of the sternomastoid muscles, the strap muscles, lay limp and useless and air bubbled out of a rent in the trachea. Wally applied encircling ligatures to both large vessels to stem the hemorrhage. It wasn't possible to repair these two important vessels, only tie them off, but Wally gambled that Tosh would still get enough blood to his brain from the carotid on the other side—if he lived, that is.

More silk thread was used to re-approximate the edges of Tosh's slashed windpipe and to cobble together the loose ends of the strap muscles. Wally would have liked to have buttressed these flimsy closings with fascia or a muscle flap but no suitable donor site was apparent. He hoped that the taut skin over Tosh's neck and an external compress would suffice to contain any further leakages he'd not dealt with.

Eventually the job was done and Wally was able to suture closed the wide opening in Tosh's neck. He doused the wound with carbolic, in true Listerian manner, and he wound a flannel bandage over a thick wad of bleached muslin, around Tosh's neck, firm but not too tight, hopefully enough to compress any oozing tissues but not to constrict the circulation to the brain. For good measure, he wound a few more layers of bandage around the little man's neck.

The little first mate lying limp on the captain's table was breathing more quietly and regularly but he had remained unconscious throughout and the blood flow to his limbs was now no more than trivial. Would he wake up? Had he sustained a major stroke? Had he lost too much blood? These questions hammered inside Wally's head.

"We'll put him in my bunk," said Wally. "I can watch him more closely there."

The men murmured assent and Trumble nodded.

They carried Tosh forward to Wally's cabin, the three men who were doing the lifting hardly able to squeeze in. They laid him down. A couple of the men, Catholics, performed the sign of the cross to invoke powers beyond what Wally could provide. Clearly something more than luck would be needed for Tosh to live out the night.

"Thanks for all your help," said Wally, rinsing off his bloodied hands in his wash bucket. The letter he'd been writing to Arthur still lay on the locker beside the bucket. He'd have something worthwhile to tell him now.

Edwards shrugged his shoulders and led the men away.

19 The Sargasso Sea

6 September. Day 20. Noon. 19.63N, 32.33W. Wind NE, moderate. Bearing 245.

The Canary Current originates at the Promontory of Sagres and runs parallel to the African coast. It continues north of the Cape Verde Islands, and becomes the North Equatorial Current, or Trade Winds, crossing the Atlantic parallel to the equator and emptying into the Caribbean Sea. Then, the Gulf Stream, like a huge river, flows back toward Europe and at the Azores branches out into the North Atlantic Current and the Canary Current. This dance of the Atlantic has not changed for thousands of years. All these currents create boundaries around a vast sea of seaweed, a sea without shores, forming the heart of the Atlantic. Centuries ago, the Portuguese christened it the Sargasso Sea.

The new morning dawned with the *Arabella* gently bobbing in thick seaweed. What little wind there'd the day been before had died and the air was hot and sticky. A pod of white-sided dolphins, two dozen or more, frolicked around the ship in the calm blue sea and some flying fish flew up onto the deck.

Little Tosh still clung to life but hadn't shown any sign of waking up. He had lost a massive amount of blood and his pulse, now palpable, was racing at a hundred and fifty a minute. One good sign was that his breathing was noticeably stronger.

Captain Trumble's task was to discover just who had been responsible—who had slashed out at Tosh and why? What an unsavory business for a ship's captain. He had enough to worry about already, without having to act as a criminal investigator. In the usual circumstances, he would have turned the job over to Tosh and been free of it. Who would help him now?

McConnochie, of course—Wally, the doctor. He'd be the ideal man to get to the bottom of this. Why, hadn't he promptly resolved the dispute between Tosh and the cook just a day ago?

Wally was tired and none too thrilled at being drawn into the investigation, but Trumble, sitting at the table where Wally had labored just hours before, would brook no disagreement.

"Who might you suspect?" the captain said. "Who could have had a hand in this?"

Wally couldn't help thinking that his friend, Arthur Conan Doyle, would've been the better man for such a task. He loved playing detective. He'd figure out those important clues that would disclose the culprit in no time at all.

"Well?" said the captain.

"It could've been any one of a number of men," said Wally.

"Such as?"

"The cook—he and Tosh don't get along."

"And?"

"Spencer, Charlie Spencer. Tosh did just hit him yesterday."

"Any more?"

Wally recalled the bizarre charcoal sketches he'd seen a few days ago. Might they be the outward sign of a frenzied killer?

"Edwards, sir. There's something a bit odd about him. He worries me."

"Well, that's a fat lot of good. Three killers when we only need one."

Wally had to agree. There had to be another clue, something that would narrow down the search.

He said, "Tosh's wound was on the right side of his neck. A man wielding a knife would have to be left handed, wouldn't he, to inflict such a wound."

"Of course, said Trumble. "I know Blodgett and Edwards are right handed, but I must say I've never taken enough notice of the Jamaican to know what hand he favors."

"But then again, the attacker might have come from behind … probably did. Tosh had no other cuts … nothing to suggest he defended himself … as he damned well would've, had he known."

"So he'd be right handed now. Is that what you're saying?" said Trumble.

"Probably."

"That's not going to get us anywhere," said Trumble in an exasperated tone. "You'll just have to interrogate the men, one by one. See what they were doing at the time. Maybe the helmsman saw someone. Start with him."

The helmsman had little to offer. Yes, he'd seen Tosh making his rounds, checking the set of the sails, seeing that all was secure on deck and—oh yes, looking for the signaling lantern. It was missing from its usual hanging place. But he'd seen no-one else in the minutes before the cry went up.

The man who discovered Tosh was an able seaman who'd been with the *Arabella* for a dozen or more years. He had been on his way for'ard to have a suck on his pipe before piling into his hammock to sleep. Some of the men objected to him smoking it in the confined space of the foc's'le and his evening foray to the bow was a long-standing tradition.

When Wally returned to his cabin to draw up a list of crew-members—it seemed he'd have to interview them all—he found his little dog, Skipper, up on the bunk licking Tosh's face. The first mate was awake, or at least with his eyes open, and he looked perplexed. His eyes darted back and forth but in every other respect he might as well have been a stuffed teddy bear, so cumbersomely did the gauze and bandages envelop his neck preventing any nod or shake of his head.

"Tosh, can you hear me?"

The answer was more of a grunt than a word, "Uurr." He may have been objecting to Skipper's ministrations.

"You're going to be all right," said Wally as he lifted Skipper down.

Wally lifted Tosh's head a little and put a mug of water to his mouth. The injured
man made a feeble attempt to sip but he couldn't free open his lips so Wally dabbed his mouth with a wet cloth.

"Can you wiggle your toes for me?"

The toes wiggled, and then his fingers—quite a relief because it meant that Tosh hadn't had a major stroke.

After an hour, Tosh was even more alert. Captain Trumble came to Wally's cabin to see the transformation for himself. Whatever

Old Bumble's faults, he was certainly concerned for the welfare of his men, and for none more than his little first mate.

"Who did this to you, Tosh? Speak, man! We have to know." Perhaps he would strike again or come back to finish Tosh off. The captain thought these things but kept them to himself.

"Mmmrrr." A grimace of pain accompanied the unintelligible mumble.

"Perhaps he could make a sign with his fingers, sir," said Wally.

"Good idea."

"Tosh, can you wiggle your fingers to say yes?" said Wally.

The fingers wiggled.

"Do you know who did it, Tosh?"

The fingers wiggled again.

"Edwards?"

No movement.

"Spencer?"

Nothing.

"Blodgett?"

Still nothing.

Trumble worked his way through the whole crew list. Mounting frustration showed on Tosh's face but his fingers did not indict anyone.

"Well, damn it, man," said Trumble, "was he not a member of the crew?" What seemed a clever method of communicating with the injured man was losing its gloss.

The fingers again didn't flicker.

"That just doesn't make sense," said Trumble, losing patience.

"There is someone we've missed,' said Wally.

"Who?"

"The Monkey!"

Tosh's fingers fluttered up a storm.

Trumble was out the cabin as if shot from a cannon. He barreled up on deck and glared up the foretop where The Monkey was huddled in his usual position.

"Get down here, right this minute!"

The Monkey moved but only to distance himself further out along the fore yard. He also drew his knife and held it ready as if to counter any man who might climb up to get him.

No amount of shouting from Trumble or the others could dislodge The Monkey from his perch. To all appearances the standoff might well last for days, until The Monkey fell from weakness or starvation. But Trumble had another idea, one that would resolve the guilty man's fate more expeditiously and would allow the ship to return to peace and calm.

Off to his cabin he went and returned with his brace of Webley pistols, the only guns allowed aboard the ship. They were percussion revolvers, capable of being loaded with five shots but they were old and no-one had used them for years. Trumble talked about them quite a deal, but whether they still worked or not was anyone's guess. A gun could easily jam if it wasn't well lubricated or if it was loaded incorrectly.

Trumble made a big show of loading one of them and all the while warning The Monkey that he was going to use it if he didn't come down to the deck that very minute. He measured out the powder and methodically filled four of the chambers, each time emphatically thrusting down the rammer, as if expending some of his pent-up anger. He pressed four lead balls in on top of the powder and checked the smooth roll of the cylinder. Slowly and carefully he capped the back of each chamber, pressing the caps in place with a dowel.

"Last chance, sir," he called, the way a man might offer his dueling partner a last way out. The Monkey shifted even further to leeward so that now it was the sea and not the deck that lay below him.

"All right then," said Trumble, and he raised the pistol with both hands and pointed the muzzle in The Monkey's direction. "You asked for it."

The gun went off with a roar and Trumble fell back onto the deck, arms and legs flying. The effect on The Monkey was no less dramatic and he plummeted down into the ocean. The fright might have done it but just as easily the lead ball might've hit him. By the time Trumble regained his feet, The Monkey had disappeared from sight and was never seen again.

"I got him, didn't I," cried Trumble. "By God, I did."

No-one chose to debate the captain's conclusion—they were just pleased the whole episode was done with. The Monkey was gone and all was well again aboard ship.

Over the next few days, Tosh regained his voice and was able to fill in the details of the night he was attacked. He'd been doing his rounds when he came upon The Monkey leaning over the starboard rail and working the shutter of the signaling lantern, no doubt sending a message to the mystery ship, in all likelihood a privateer. In the tussle that followed, The Monkey pulled a knife and slashed out at him. The last thing he could remember was feeling a bolt of lightning in his neck, or at least that's what it felt like at the time.

Now the mystery ship had disappeared. It was highly unlikely that The Monkey had been picked up—he'd probably swum about for a few hours until he tired and sank beneath the waves. Nobody aboard the *Arabella* gave him a moments more thought, except Wally who described the incident in great detail in his letter to Arthur. That, and the matter of the growing number of mosquitoes, filled a full five pages of quarto.

20   The Leeward Islands

21 September. Day 35. Noon. 17.54N, 59.87W. Wind ENE, light. Bearing 270.

The weather in early summer is usually quite predictable in the mid-Atlantic and so it proved on this trip, an occasional thunderstorm or a pocket of calm but for the most part moderate favorable winds and dry, sunny conditions. The ocean was at peace, a boon for the *Arabella* because it was a ship that needed cosseting. Even Trumble's tribulations wielding the sextant caused him less distress—no clouds obscured the noon sun and no waves pitched the deck about.

Tosh's neck was badly swollen but it was healing and showed no sign of infection, and the other men were all in good health. Wally had little to do, other than read snatches out of *The Tale of Two Cities* and try to teach Skipper a trick or two. The little dog could jump and catch a stick, and occasionally he'd even return it. Life was easy, those days, and Wally relaxed into a state of contentment.

Not so for the older hands aboard who went about their routine with an air of watchful anticipation. They worked the ship, reefing and furling, knotting and splicing, standing their watch and taking a trick at the wheel, always with an eye to the sky and a cheek to the wind. No following breeze noticeably brightened them nor did any sunshine seem to cause them joy. They knew the power of the sea, its sudden switches in mood and how often a calm precedes a storm.

The morning Captain Trumble called the men to the deck the wily ones had a good idea what he was going to tell them.

"Tomorrow we should be seeing land—Antigua—and we'll put in at English Harbour." Antigua, Caribbean base for the British Navy during Nelson's time, was one of the Leeward Islands, a chain of luxuriant islets that stretched across the path of any ship riding the trades to Jamaica. The Dutch, the French and the British had each bagged their own, creating havens where they could come ashore and replenish their supplies of meat and vegetables: oases of land on a desert of sea. In these remote outposts of Empire, one could expect food prepared in the national style—roast beef with Yorkshire pudding in Antigua, pickled herring in Curacao—and mail could be sent home with a reasonable expectation of delivery.

"And I can have me a taste of milky possett and a noggin," said the helmsman. He was the only man who didn't take a drop of alcohol at sea but he drank more than most when on dry land, a mixture of eggs, milk and ale being his favorite.

"A proper skin-full, more like," piped in one of the boys, loud enough for all to hear. A cackle of laughter ran around the assembled crew.

"Dammit! Listen to me," said Trumble, gruffly. "Before any man is allowed ashore, we'll have full clearance from the quarantine officer. We've had no fevers this voyage, so far, and I intend to keep it that way. If any ship is flying the yellow jack, or if I even hear about one, we'll lay off up the coast and take provisions from ashore."

The seriousness of the fever threat lowered a gloom over the men. Trumble didn't need to remind them of the calamity experienced by the *Arabella* crew on their last visit to the Caribbean.

"And," he added, "I'm ordering Doctor McConnochie to give every attention to the daily reports issued by the Quarantine Office. The first hint of a fever and we leave immediately."

"Yes, sir," said Wally. He'd already planned a visit to the Quarantine Office but he suspected that by the time an outbreak was posted it would be too late to escape scot-free. Yellow fever spread through a port with the speed of a locomotive, and just as quickly struck down those who lay in its track. Nobody really knew what signs to look for and the only forecasts of an impending epidemic came from fortune-tellers, shamans, soothsayers and other hucksters of quackery. A prophecy based on science would have to wait until the mode of transmission was established and that didn't appear to be any time soon.

As the *Arabella* edged into the mouth of the protected bay that was English Harbour, all eyes scanned the foremasts of the other ships for pennants. Some flags were pointed, some square, and many were colored. Wally could recognize only a handful. He knew the a red swallow-tailed burgee signaled that a ship had explosives on board and that a blue flag with a white square in the center, the Blue Peter, meant the vessel was about to sail. He was pleased to see no sign of the square black and yellow checkered flag which a ship must fly in port if they had a dangerous infection aboard.

"Looks clear, Tosh," he said to his now much-recovered friend.

"Aye, for the moment, but best we keep our fingers crossed. A change of wind could flush the devil out." Tosh's close call with death had left him despondent and cynical, as if the knife that struck him had gouged away the jaunty cockiness that had been his hallmark. In his sleep he was dogged by assassins lurking in dark shadows and, by day, his gait was cautious and a mite unsteady. He now avoided going aloft.

"And take your little mutt with you," he added, without humor. The sight of three-legged Skipper unsettled Tosh as much as anything did, as if the maimed dog reminded him of his own burden of instability.

The ship dropped anchor in the shadow of Shirley Heights, a great promontory that overlooked the picturesque cove. The hills afforded excellent protection from the wind and the waters there could be flat as glass when it was blowing a gale on the open sea a half mile to the west. Of course, the lack of any breeze could work against a sailboat, especially one as doddery as the *Arabella*, and the services of a small steam tug were needed to help maneuver the old ship to a suitable berth.

The ship's longboat was lowered from the davits and a couple of oarsmen rowed Wally, Skipper and Captain Trumble over to the merchants' dock. A rather makeshift-looking wooden hut, the dock master's office, sat at the end of the wharf and a large green parrot was perched on a brass ring hanging from the door jam.

"Back again? I though you was packin' it in," said the dock master, a shriveled-up old Cockney who'd lived most of his life in the islands.

"Gaaarrrkkk," screeched his parrot, as if to concur.

"Aha, don't you gimme no lip," said Trumble with a smile, but whether he was talking to the dock master, the parrot or both,

Wally couldn't tell. He could see, however, that the two men were good friends—a relationship of the type forged through sharing the anxieties and losses that the wild forces of the Caribbean can pile on a man. Not all of these forces were created by the sea; some of the worst were a product of the dregs of humankind that scavenged around the island ports: thieves, thugs, bullies and blackguards. Some were black, most were white; all had shoe leather for skin and no more moral fiber than a brick. Years of facing off against such scum, on ships and on land, made a man more appreciative of his true friends. Wally could see the two of them having a meal together and sharing a bottle of rum, this night or on the morrow—that is, if the fever demon didn't raise his vicious head.

"And this is Dr McConnochie—Wally, we call him. He'll be wanting to check in at the quarantine office."

"Things have been quiet on that front, for a month or more," said the dock master, eyeing over Wally and the dog. He threw a piece of biscuit to Skipper.

"I can take him over but I'll be right back. Put on the kettle if you like."

Trumble led Wally along the dock to a stone building with big white wooden shutters and a Union Jack hanging limp on a pole mounted above the doorway. The plinking sound of someone playing the piano—not very well—emanated from within.

"That'll be Stanley, the Quarantine Officer," said Trumble. "He plays the piano by ear and as often as not he sings along with it."

"Doesn't it irritate people? He's playing off key."

"No, they don't mind his playing. In fact they like it."

"Really?"

"Mostly because it means he's not busy. There can't be any fever about."

Stanley was a tall, thin man with grey hair and big ears that stuck out like studs'ls. His face was creased with wrinkles. He shook Wally by the hand and listened to Trumble's introduction of the young doctor.

"It's years since I was in Glasgow," Stanley said. "For a time, my father had a butcher shop on the Byres Road. We went back down to Portsmouth after that. Too bloody cold, that Scotland."

"And wet," said Wally.

"But here, you're from somewhere else, yourself."

"New Zealand," said Wally.

"And a touch of aborigine in you."

"Maori. I'm half Maori, sir."

"Ah, there's a difference, is there? Well, to me it's how you act, not how you look, that's important. The same's true for sailors, isn't it Captain?"

Trumble nodded and turned towards the door.

"I'll leave you two to talk," he said and he strode off back in the direction of the dock master's hut.

The Quarantine man sat Wally down and asked him if he'd been in the tropics before and whether he'd ever seen a case of yellow fever or malaria. On learning that Wally hadn't, he braced his shoulders back and took on the superior air of a lecturer, a role he'd obviously practiced, but like his piano playing, had not yet fully got right.

"Well, young man, I mayn't have a degree but I dare say that I've had more exposure to the damnable Barbados fever than any white man alive. I'm a scholar of experience and not averse to sharing my hard-won wisdom with another man of medicine. Might a guinea be a reasonable investment for the chance to save your shipmates' lives?"

The temerity of a public official asking to be paid extra for doing his appointed job annoyed Wally, but this was a man not to be dismissed lightly. What he knew might be of critical importance to the health of the crew.

"I have no money with me, sir, but I'm sure I could prevail on Captain Trumble for the guinea. I'll chase right after him, now."

Stanley seemed a little startled at that idea. "No, no, there's no need for that," he blurted, with a dismissive wave of a hand. And, after a pause, he said, "I have a better idea. I'll tell it you for free."

"For free?"

"Yes, on condition you come again tomorrow and attend a friend of mine. He's very sick and needs a surgeon. You'll understand, I think, when you see him."

"I'll do my best," said Wally. He could see that the Quarantine Officer's request would have to be met if he was to learn anything new about yellow fever.

With the negotiation settled, Stanley visibly relaxed. He returned to the piano and sat before it.

"Do you play?" he said.

"No," said Wally.

"What would you like to hear?" said Stanley, spreading his long fingers over the keyboard.

"Nothing right now, Nothing at all. I'll be back again tomorrow ... in the morning. All right?"

"Oh yes, sometime before noon. My friend'll be here."

As Wally walked, and Skipper hobbled, away from the big stone building with its white shutters, he could hear Stanley plinking away at the piano. The tune was an old concert hall favorite, *The Galloping Major*, but Stanley's flawed rendition turned it into a caricature—much as Stanley was himself.

Skipper accompanied Wally when he retraced his steps to the Quarantine Office the next morning. They made an odd couple, the tall brown doctor with a tattoo scarred on his chest and the three-legged dog. But no-one seemed to notice. Here in the Islands oddities were commonplace; it was the lack of them that raised an eye-brow.

Stanley was all smiles and offered a handful of dried beef to Skipper.

"Top o' the mornin' to you, Doc."

"And to you, sir," said Wally.

"I'd like you to meet my friend, Albert. He's not up to it just now, but when he's in proper fettle he's the best banjo player in the whole of Antigua."

Albert gave a wry smile. Even sitting as he was, on the other side of the room, Albert looked uncomfortable. His belly was so distended that he was forced to sprawl across the divan, resting on his elbows. His ankles were grotesquely swollen and weeping with watery fluid. These things Wally observed with clinical detachment but what did surprise him was that Albert was an African, as black as coal, and the whites of his eyes weren't white at all—they were bright yellow.

"Albert is a minister, over at Cobbs Cross—where our hardest-working boys come from."

It didn't matter that Wally hadn't heard of the settlement a mile or so from English Harbour—he could imagine the place: a cluster of dirty shacks, thatched walls and rusty tin roofs, a dog outside and maybe a pig or a goat, much like his own village at Otakau, the one he'd left to go to school in Dunedin. Singing and drinking rum would be the best these folk—these boys—could look forward to, and to be so lucky they'd have to labor long and hard under demanding white overseers: cutting sugar cane, hauling logs for settlers' houses and breaking rocks for building roads. A minister's job was to remind them of their obligation to do the white man's bidding. Should they slacken they'd be thrown out of the camp and lose whatever few shillings their back-breaking toil had earned them. The *blackbirders* in Queensland were much the same—natives from New Hebrides or the Solomons, kidnapped and forced to work in Australia's sugar plantations until they dropped, and all for a pittance, many of them tricked into boarding the kidnap ships by dishonest native ministers who brokered them away for a bounty.

He kept a stiff face to hide the repugnance he felt for such men.

"And what's your main problem?" he said, addressing the minister.

"Main problem? That would have to be my wife."

Wally didn't laugh. He was impatient with the manner adopted by many of the downtrodden to hide all of life's miseries beneath a veneer of clever banter and clichéd jokes.

"Tell him about your swelling," interrupted Stanley, his voice gentle and reassuring.

"Main *medical* problem," said Wally, for clarification. He already suspected cirrhosis of the liver, the outcome of too many binges on the rum he'd procured with his tainted income.

"My belly's all swollen up. It's been getting worse for months but now I can't even sit up straight and I can't stand for long either."

"And what have other doctors said?"

"He's not seen another doctor," said Stanley.

"Oh, and why not," said Wally. A minister and a manager of cheap labor—he should be able to afford any one of a number of doctors, local or visiting off a ship.

"We can talk about it later, Wally, but suffice it to say that Albert is none too popular around here. You see, he thinks his people should get better pay and better living conditions and he's willing to fight for it. The animosity of the landowners is such that Albert is a wanted man. I had to smuggle him in to see you here today."

"Don't get into all that, Mister Stanley," said Albert, reaching down to pat Skipper on the head.

"Not all his people agree with him either, least of all his wife. They're scared, you see."

"What would they do to you?"

"The last man was lynched," said Albert. "He was a cousin of mine and he didn't watch his back. However we're stronger now. I think Mister Stanley is exaggerating."

"But surely the doctors here shouldn't pick and chose who they help," said Wally.

"They're all white and they stick to their own," said Stanley.

"Anyway them white doctors don't know how to cure us colored folk. We're different, aren't we, Doc?" Albert gave a deep laugh and his belly wobbled, no doubt with all the fluid in it sloshing around.

"Lie back then, Albert, and let me take a closer look at you," said Wally.

He peered into Albert's eyes and he checked the fullness of the veins in his neck. He percussed Albert's bloated belly and he prodded him for lumps and masses. He placed his ear over Albert's heart and listened for murmurs and extra sounds. All these things he did, yet he learned no more than he'd already guessed when he walked into the room.

"You have a liver problem, my man," he said. "And I suspect it comes from drink."

"But that's not possible," said Albert. "I never touch a drop."

"Neither he has," echoed Stanley.

"I seen what it does to people," said Albert.

"Well, maybe we don't know the cause, but it's your liver sure enough," said Wally.

"Can you do anything, Doc?" said Stanley.

"I can take off some of the fluid. Maybe that'll help him feel easier … for now, at least."

"Oh, do it! Do it, please," said Albert.

"I'll have to bring some things from the ship," said Wally. "Can you look after Skipper till I get back."

"He'll be treated like a king," said Stanley, reaching for the can that held the dried beef. "Take my dory."

Rowing back to the *Arabella*, Wally reflected on the inaccuracy of his first impressions. He'd been completely wrong to think of Albert as a rum-soaked white man's lackey. The very thing that he found fault with in others, he'd done himself. The next time someone makes a faux pas about his own brown color or his big tattoo—a joke, a snide remark—he should let it just wash over him. We can all make mistakes.

He rummaged through his velvet-lined box of surgical instruments, pushing aside the elevators, forceps, tenacula and saws. All he really needed was his chrome-plated trocar and a scalpel. He wished he had some ethyl chloride to use as an anesthetic but it was too volatile to travel well on a ship in the tropics. He spotted the shiny brass endotracheal tube that Doctor Macewen had given him, but he shook his head. To give old Albert chloroform might do him more harm than good. He might never wake up.

He chose not to tell Captain Trumble what he was about; after all, this little procedure was taking place on land, not aboard the ship, and Trumble's authority counted for nothing in the Quarantine Office. In a way, he was doing this to help the captain and the crew. Hadn't he been told to get in good standing with the Quarantine man? What better way to do it?

Albert was lying flat on the divan, his boots off and his shirt still unbuttoned. His eyes opened wider when he saw the sharp-pointed trocar, its shaft as thick as his thumb, which was to be thrust into his abdomen.

"Will I feel it?" he said.

"Only for a second," said Wally. And, addressing Stanley, he said, "I want you to hold Albert's hands up over his head—to stretch the skin where I'll be working. Hold 'em up there firmly and don't let go, you hear!"

Albert's belly was taut as a drum already, but his hands might flail around with the shock of the scalpel incision or the forceful introduction of the trocar. A man in pain, even a very sick man, could become a monster and a smart surgeon took precautions to protect himself from being attacked.

Wally rubbed some carbolic on the skin below the navel and positioned his instruments within easy reach—speed was important when no anesthetic was available. The scalpel went in and Albert let out a cry.

"Hold on tight, Stanley!" cried Wally, and with a quick movement he plunged the trocar into the wound and down through the peritoneal membrane. The gush of fluid was instantaneous and profuse. It spilled out, soaking Albert's clothes and the divan, and it poured down onto the floor to form a large red puddle.

"I'm sorry," said Wally. "I should've known there'd be a flood."

"That's of no consequence," said Stanley. "The main thing is for Albert to get better."

Bloody ascitic fluid drained out of the trocar for twenty minutes and Albert's heaving belly deflated along with it. No pus issued out, which was good, but the sight of the blood raised the specter of more ominous diagnoses in Wally's mind. A cancer or sarcoma had probably invaded Albert's liver and may even have spread to other organs. The poor minister would likely need spiritual help more than he'd need medicine.

Albert did feel much improved, once the trocar was removed and he'd exchanged his soggy britches for a pair of Stanley's trousers. He demonstrated to them how he could now sit up straight, bend over, even reach down and roll up the cuffs of his borrowed pants. He beamed like a boy with a new pony.

"I knew you'd be the man for him," said Stanley, signaling a new level in their relationship.

True to his word, the Quarantine man spent the next hour tutoring Wally on what he knew about yellow fever. The headache, fever, lemon-colored skin and black vomit, Wally had heard about from his friend, Patrick Manson, but to talk to someone who'd seen dozens of cases was enlightening.

"The Spanish call it *vomito negro* because of the black muddy stuff the sorry victims bring up."

"I'm more interested in the cause?" Wally said. "Where do you think the yellow fever comes from?"

"Bad air," said Stanley, "the same bad air that brings malaria can breed yellow fever. I think yellow fever is a form of malaria, a special strain of the dreaded disease that's adapted itself to the tropics and, what's worse, to certain ships. There's a devil's curse on places like Antigua and Kingston and it was shared by the *Flying Dutchman* and other sorry ships like it."

"You know the *Arabella* had a bad outbreak on the last trip?" said Wally.

"I heard as much. Even more reason that you take heed and plan accordingly."

"But what on earth can I do? What can anybody do?"

"Well, for a start, you might as well use your Maori mumbo-jumbo as any of the medicines you have aboard: your calomel, your antimony and your Epsom salts—all just as futile as bloodletting or blistering."

"Jalap and mercury?" said Wally.

"A waste of time."

"Quinine? If yellow fever's a form of malaria, shouldn't that help?"

"It's not the same. Yellow fever is so much more virulent that quinine doesn't touch it."

"I've been told that the humble mosquito might carry the disease around," said Wally. "It could inject a victim when it bites him."

"Another hare-brained notion, I'm sure," said Stanley. "Someone comes up with another foolish explanation every month. We've pointed the finger at blacks, Chinese, immigrants of all races. Others claim the disease is spread by birds, roaches or rats. Even dogs have been singled out. Some say it's floating in the air or hiding in the garbage, spread by a sneeze or contact with vomit. Whole ship-loads of coffee have been cast into the sea for fear that yellow fever was hiding inside the sacks. When nobody knows the cause, everyone and everything is suspected."

"Well, what would you suggest I do if an attack strikes the *Arabella*. I can't just stand by and do nothing."

"Open all the hatches and let good fresh air circulate through-out the ship. I'd start with that. Then I'd clean the ship of filth, stem to stern: scrub the decks, throw all the garbage overboard, maybe even burn some sulfur or tobacco. Pump the bilge out, too."

"If we have enough hands available, that is!"

"And do it early on. Give the beast enough slack and he'll soon overwhelm you."

Albert, who had been resting quietly chimed in, "And say your prayers, doc. That's another thing you should do. All the men should."

"I appreciate the advice," said Wally, but the prospect of being so impotent in the face of a virulent outbreak of fever took the wind out of his sails. He gave a long sigh. Relying on prayer was not a sturdy shield with which to enter battle.

Wally beckoned Skipper, now done eating his dried beef, and said goodbye to Albert and Stanley.

"I look forward to seeing both of you again next time I'm in Antigua."

"I invite you to our village," said Albert. "We have the best akee and salt fish on the whole island." Wally would like that, but in his heart he suspected that the minister's days were numbered.

"Remember what I told you," said Stanley, waving his index finger in a paternal kind of way.

Wally and Skipper made their way back to the dock, Wally kicking at imaginary stones and Skipper looking out for other dogs. It would be their last moment of freedom before they were holed up in the ship again. Not that he planned to run away, but Wally would have preferred to be in a place where he could. Aboard the *Arabella*, there was no escape.

New come Buckra,
He get sick;
He tak Fever,
He be die,
He be die.

19th Century Jamaican song (*Buckra* refers to a white man).

True to his word, Trumble gave the order to weigh anchor the next morning. Fresh provisions had been loaded and the mail had been dispatched, including Wally's letter to Arthur. To loiter in Antigua was to invite trouble, not only from yellow fever but also from venereal disease, brawling and desertion. For a ship's captain, the most worrying time was when the ship was in port. At sea, the elements might be fickle, even downright dangerous, but there the men were under his control and he had the lash and the irons to back him up.

The effect of receiving a letter from a friend or a loved one varied. Sometimes it led to high spirits and the anticipation of going home; at other times, it served as a bitter reminder of family illness or lack of money. Wally did not receive a letter from Doyle, a disappointment, but perhaps one would be waiting for him in Kingston. Mail was haphazard in most parts of the world and especially in the Caribbean, liable to the whims of the shipping agent, the timing of mail ships and the conscientiousness of poorly-paid colonial postal clerks. That any mail did reach the ship was a miracle in itself.

Trumble set a westerly course for Jamaica, passing to the north of friendly Montserrat and keeping well to the south of Santo

Domingo, home port to some of the most cut-throat pirates in the Antilles. Had all been well, the trip should've taken less than a week. But life at sea is never certain.

The first sign of a problem was Tosh banging on Wally's cabin door at four bells into the morning watch, two days out from Antigua.

"Doc, come quick! We have a veritable situation on our hands." Tosh was hopping from one foot to the other, his whole body atremble.

"Speak clearly, man. What are you referring to?"

"It's Mister Mudd, Doc, he's taken an awful turn."

And so he had. Joshua Mudd was an American by birth, but he'd sailed on British ships for years. He was one of the new crew Trumble had hired in Liverpool and he'd proved himself a worthy jack-tar, some days pitching in with the reefing and furling and on others taking his hand at the wheel or helping in the galley. He led a little prayer service on deck each Sunday, reciting lines from the Bible and singing a hymn or two, hence his being called Reverend by some or simply Mister by others, a sign of respect usually reserved for the first mate.

He would not be working the sheets this day, however. He twisted and turned in his hammock as if lying on a bed of hot coals; his eyes were wild and his mouth open in a silent scream; a thin stream of blood trickled from his nose. The enemy had arrived and had laid claim to his first victim.

Tosh looked up at Wally.

"Is it what I think, Doc?" he whispered.

"Do the men know?"

"Of course they know."

"And the Captain?"

"Water! Give me some water, for heaven's sake." Joshua Mudd's rasping voice interrupted their hushed exchange.

"We'll get you some, Joshua," said Wally and he motioned for Tosh to follow him up the companionway to the deck.

The conference with Captain Trumble was uncomfortable for all concerned. Trumble knew only too well how devastating an outbreak of yellow fever could be—so did Tosh—and Wally sensed that he was soon to find out. Trumble was still in his bunk in his night gown, the cloth cap on his head looking comical under less troubling circumstances. His bared teeth gnawed away at his clenched fist but no crisp order was forthcoming.

"I'd like to suggest we move on the offensive, sir," said Wally. If Trumble was going to dither then it would be up to him to take the lead.

"Oh sure," said the captain. "And how do we fight this enemy, this infernal devil that you've never crossed before?"

"Clear the ship of mosquitoes, sir. That'd be my first step."

The captain yanked off his nightcap and threw it on the floor. "Jesus! I get a lunatic for a doctor! You hear what he said, Mister Mitford?"

"Sir, listen to him," said Tosh. "It does sound irregular ..."

"Irregular? Irregular! My god, *crazy*, more like. We got a fight on our hands and all I hear about is clearing the ship of harmless mosquitoes."

"We could start with that, sir," said Wally. "I can't guarantee anything but it's worth a shot. Better than what you did last time perhaps."

This last comment brought the distracted captain to a stop. He turned and looked straight at Wally, as if seeing him for the first time.

"Explain yourself," he said. "And it better be good."

Wally described Patrick Manson's theory in a way that made it seem almost fact. If he could gain the captain's confidence only by a slight twisting of the truth, then that's what he'd do. This was not a time for clean scientific objectivity; it was a time for dirty science, the kind that politician's use when they want to get their way. Manson had better be right because, if he wasn't, men were going to die.

When Wally had finished his spirited pitch, Trumble turned and looked out the porthole.

"A'right then," he said. "We'll start with a fumigation but we also get rid of the dog and the parrot."

Wally stepped forward with a start.

"What? But sir, Skipper doesn't have anything to do with the fever."

"And a mosquito does?"

"I don't see any need—"

"McConnochie! That's an order."

"But, sir—"

"Out, dammit! I have things to do."

Tosh half led, half pulled Wally out of the captain's cabin.

"No point antagonizing him, Doc. His mind's made up for once. And don't worry, sir, I know you love that dog. I'll hide him down below under the knight-heads. The Old Man never goes down there."

The mixture of anger and sadness that Wally felt that morning was not going to leave him for quite some time. What he couldn't know then was that both Skippers were the least of his problems.

27 September. Day 41. Noon. 16.44N, 72.64W. Wind SE, moderate. Bearing 270.

The ship was fumigated with burning sulfur, not once but three times, and still mosquitoes remained.

"They seem to like the stink of sulfur," said Samuel Edwards, the carpenter.

"We should pump the bilge again, too," said Wally.

The two men had become closer friends these last few days ever since Edwards offered to help out tending to the sick man, Mudd.

At first, Wally was leery of the carpenter's intentions. Hadn't he seen him drawing macabre scenes of blacks being set upon by whites? He even confronted Edwards.

"I thought you didn't like darkies?" he said, late one evening, as they sat in the fo'c'sle, Mudd breathing stertorously behind them.

"No. What gave you that idea?"

"Your pictures. The drawings you do."

"Oh, them."

Edwards paused to make a frown.

"Them are drawings about nightmares I have," he continued. "I dream horrible things and I draw them on a page so that I can crumple 'em up and throw 'em away. It helps, you know."

"So you've got nothing against a colored man, a wog, a darkie, even a mulatto?" This *mulatto* term Wally had heard bandied about in Antigua—it meant *man of mixed race.*

"No, you—they—can't help it—just like your dog. He didn't ask to be an oddity, just like a Chink or an Aborigine didn't plan themselves to be neither. And the same's the thing for a dwarf or a cretin, for that matter."

"But you think all those people are oddities, though."

"We're all a bit odd. Just in different ways," said the carpenter. "I'm odd, you're odd. We're all bloody odd."

"You mean with your nightmares?"

"No, lots of folk have *them*."

"Well, how are you odd?"

"I don't have no parents."

"Of course you must. You were born, weren't you?"

"Nobody knows who my dad was, and my mum, when I was a baby, she left me with her parents and skipped town. I never seen neither one of 'em in me whole life."

Wally shrugged. He couldn't think of anything useful to say. What help would it be to Edwards to tell him how lucky he might've been *not* to know his parents. How fortunate not to have a father who'd committed murder or a mother who people laughed and pointed at. He could make his parents be anyone he wanted.

Behind them the noisy breathing had stopped. The Reverend Mr Mudd was dead and neither Wally nor Edwards had noticed.

"*Aue*, and here we are talking drivel," said Wally, distressed by his neglect of doctoring duties. Yet in a way it was a relief. He had nothing left to offer Mr Mudd and his inadequacy deeply disturbed him. Now he could concentrate on his number one enemy, the mosquito.

Many factors make a mosquito an ideal killing machine. First of all he is hard to see. He's small, moves very quickly and he does his dirty work at night. During the day he hides in the most inaccessible parts of a ship, no doubt discussing battle plans with his fellow combatants. Secondly his instrument of attack is a needle-sharp proboscis strategically positioned out front so as to strike like a spear as he dives into his victim. Manson would have it that the yellow fever organism is squirted out through that proboscis, like a poison dart ejected from the blow-pipe of a Dayak tribesman from Borneo. The third, and perhaps most devastating, advantage that the mosquito has is that he can reproduce himself every day or two. More aerial attack troops can be amassed in next to no time. The poor sailors are outnumbered from day one, but the odds against them climb each time the ship's bell rings.

"Mudd is gone. Now what, Doctor?" The captain spoke as if the yellow fever was a problem that belonged only to Wally. He would be the scapegoat, the one who would be blamed if things went downhill.

"We still haven't got rid of all the mosquitoes, sir," said Wally.

"You're still not on about that, are you? We've done more than any ship can do. The fumigations, the bilges, what more do you want?"

"The men could sleep out on deck, sir. The mosquitoes keep below so the men might be safer topsides. And we could try swatting them whenever we see one."

The captain was lukewarm in his support. "You can tell the men yourself, Doctor. I'll call them all on deck at four bells this afternoon."

The men were no less skeptical when they heard Wally's plan. Had the captain stood behind him or offered some inducement, perhaps Wally could've won over more, but for now he'd have to be happy that half the crew grudgingly opted to sleep on deck, at least for a few nights, and then only if wasn't raining.

For three days there were no more cases of fever, but on the fourth Charlie Spencer, one of those who'd been sleeping down in the foc's'le, fell sick. His normally-lively black face sagged and his eyes were suffused with the redness of high fever. He huddled himself into a corner of the galley on a makeshift bed of a couple of empty potato sacks.

"Come back down to the foc's'le, Charlie," said Wally. "I can tend to you better there."

"I wanna stay here."

"But you need to be bedded in a hammock. It's like an oven in here. No place for a sick man."

"I'm not going."

"Please!"

"No, no, no!"

"You must follow the doctor's orders, Charlie," said Trumble, peering into the galley.

Charlie just looked away and drew his legs up like a hedgehog rolling itself into a ball. He mumbled some words in a dialect that sounded vaguely familiar though Wally could not make sense of any one word.

"Like I said, his mind is going," Wally whispered to the captain.

"Silly local rubbish, more like. But we can't let the food get contaminated," said Trumble.

"I can make a bed up for him out on the deck," said Wally.

"Suit yourself, but do it quick," snapped the captain.

Wally enlisted Tosh's help in arranging a nest of old sailcloth for Charlie to lie on amidships. To keep out the elements they stretched more sailcloth over a length of line to form a tent and they assisted the sick man shuffle into his snug new sickbay.

"You like it?" said Wally.

"Yeah. No mosquitoes get in here?"

"No. No, they won't."

Wally hadn't thought about that before. Perhaps if the men were to isolate themselves from mosquitoes, by hiding under a covering of some sort, they might well avoid being bitten. Thick clothing and blankets would make sleep impossible in the hot and stuffy foc's'le but a tent arrangement might do the trick. Could it be a chink in the enemy's armor, a weakness of his that could be exploited?

"Land, ho!" The cry from the helmsman signaled that Jamaica was in sight. By nightfall they would be lying off Kingston but flying the dreaded yellow jack and obliged to stay offshore in quarantine, a circumstance that none of them welcomed.

"I'll be home by tomorrow," said Charlie, not acknowledging his perilous condition, or perhaps already a little delirious.

"Yes, you will," said Wally. To himself he added, "One way or another."

24 *Quarantine*

Old Bumble sat at his chart table fussing with a pile of maps. The discussion with the quarantine official had been predictable. They could enter the harbor in two weeks time but only if no new cases of fever broke out. Until a few years ago they would've had to wait forty days, such was the fear of transmitting the disease. However recent admiralty data indicated an incubation period of not longer than week, making it therefore safe to say that a ship was in the clear if it was fever-free for a fortnight.

"At least our cargo isn't perishable. It could wait a year. But can we? You know they used to call the Caribbean the white man's grave?" he said.

"Tell me more about the cargo, sir," said Wally.

"Well, linens and cottons can keep, can't they?"

"And muslin? Do we carry any muslin?"

"I suppose so. I'd have to look at the manifest. What is it to you?"

"I'd like to have some, if I may."

"Out here? Wait till you're home. It's cheaper."

"No, I mean to use it as a guard against the mosquitoes."

"Not that again! Leave off that stupid talk."

"Humor me on this, sir. Think of the needless loss if I am right and you'd not listened."

The tactic was a good one. Trumble liked to doubt his own judgment and Wally could exploit that weakness to advantage.

"You can have a bolt of muslin but God help you if it's a waste. You'll pay for it out of your earnings."

"It'll work, sir. I'm sure of it," said Wally, unable to suppress a smile.

"You think you can twist me around your little finger, McConnochie. Well, you can't. And you better let Mister Mitford break the seal on the cargo. It wouldn't look good for the doctor to be messing about down there by himself."

The aft hatch cover over the cargo hold was held secure by a large steel padlock inscribed with the words Hobbs and Co. London. Tosh used the captain's key to open it and then he and Wally dragged back the heavy wooden cover.

In the bright sunlight the neatly-stacked and colorful bolts of cloth looked like gigantic sticks of rock candy, a child's fantasy of heaven, perhaps, if one could ignore the cloying smell of camphor from a hundred thousand mothballs.

"You can see why the agent wants this kept locked," said Wally. Had it not been, pilfered cargo would have been sold or bartered at every port along their course.

They lowered themselves down into the hold.

"The muslin should be back here," said Tosh as he stepped over the lashings that held the big rolls in place. "It'll be covered with sackcloth."

Back in the shadows under the deck it was harder to see, and caution obliged them not to carry a lantern for fear they'd set the lot afire. Tosh sliced through a few stout lengths of twine and rolled some of the bolts back to expose the lower layers.

"Hey, what's this," he said.

"Where?" said Wally, peering beyond where the first mate stood.

"Jesus! It's a bloody armory," added Tosh. "Here look."

A ray of sunlight flashed a glint off the barrels of more than a couple of dozen rifles that had been discreetly hidden beneath the topmost cargo.

Wally reached down and picked one up. It wasn't new but it was well kept and had a slick coating of oil to protect against rust in a salty environment. He had seen this model before, out in the gold-fields in New Zealand. A local policeman, a man called Petrie, had one and he used sit outside his hut polishing it whenever official business was slack, admittedly not often. A couple of times, he and Wally took potshots at logs floating down the Clutha river, shrieking with pleasure when a hit blasted a gaping hole in the imaginary battleship trying to escape, not entirely correct protocol for a member of the New Zealand Armed Constabulary but an essential release for both men hemmed in, as they were those days, by occupation and circumstance.

The rifle was a standard British issue, a Martini-Henry, hammerless and with a two-piece stock. A cocking lever was hinged behind the trigger guard and above it, on the right side, sat the cocking indicator. The steel plating on the side bore a set of markings: a large crown, the letters V.R. standing for Victoria Regina, the name Enfield for the location of the Royal Armoury where it was manufactured, and the date below, 1873, told when. The Roman numeral I showed it to be a Mark I, an older model but still a powerful enforcer and, a decade earlier, standard issue for all British infantry fighting in Africa and on the Indian sub-continent.

"Who the hell do these belong to?" said Tosh.

"They're not on the bill of lading, I take it," answered Wally.

"Hell no! And old Bumble doesn't know of them. I can swear to that."

"Let's get the muslin out first—before we tell him, don't you think?" said Wally. There was no knowing what the captain would do once he'd been apprised of this new development.

In silence, the two men lifted aside the rifles and twenty boxes of .45 caliber ammunition to reveal the sacking-covered bolts of muslin.

"Just a couple should be sufficient," said Wally.

Each bolt was five feet long and held fifty yards of material. They were heavy and the two men, tall Wally and midget Tosh, labored to drag the heavy rolls up onto the deck and into the camphor-free sunlight.

Old Bumble was uncharacteristically certain when confronted with the news that the *Arabella* was carrying contraband weapons.

"Another uprising of the natives! I could smell it last time I was down here."

He went on to describe the simmering tensions that existed between the blacks and the whites here in Jamaica. A rebellious outburst had exploded a few years back at a place called Morant Bay and a handful of white farmers and dozens of blacks had been killed. Some blamed it on exploitation, others on native savagery; neither side trusted the other, then or now, and both sides were preparing for the worst.

Wally said nothing. He'd learned not to offer opinions on matters of blacks versus whites. Yet he knew it was only desperation that would lead a group of downtrodden unfortunates to rise up against their white overlords. Hadn't the same thing happened in New Zealand just a few years ago—at Poverty Bay, where Te Kooti led his Hau-Hau comrades on a rampage of death and destruction, massacring settlers, skirmishing with the militia and executing several Army officers who tried to resist? The issue there was perceived injustice over land use, failure to comply with the Treaty of Waitangi and a general lack of respect for Maori customs. Was it so different here in Jamaica, or anywhere else, for that matter?

His brown skin labeled him as lacking objectivity in any argument on these matters. That worked both ways. He was too dark for whites and too light for Maori. Neither side felt they could trust him. That, too would be the same in Jamaica and aboard a ship. So he kept his mouth shut.

Trumble paced around his cabin. He stroked his chin and he muttered to himself. Wally had never seen him so deep in concentration. Clearly, having contraband rifles aboard was more of a burden for the captain than being plagued with yellow fever. The former fell under his jurisdiction, the latter was an act of God. No matter the size of the threat or the number of lives at risk, or lost, a captain in the merchant marine, just like any politician, can keep his head held high if he follows his standing orders and the instructions of the ship's agents. Rogue rifles didn't sit well with the company directors back in Leadenhall Street.

"Blacks helped load the ship, didn't they," he said, at last. "That'll be the link. No white man needs to smuggle a rifle."

Wally again kept his own counsel. He knew, of course, that in New Zealand most purveyors of illicit goods—drugs, guns and the like—were whiter than Bumble himself. They did it for the money, a tempting influence almost unknown amongst colored people but one that shaped the very soul of Europeans.

The captain's next step in logic was quite predictable.

"Charlie, that nigger Charlie, he'll be in on it, for sure. I never trusted him, never did. Should've listened to myself. You can't trust any of those buggers." He looked at Wally, then quickly looked away.

"We should talk to him, sir," said Tosh.

"He's too sick just now," said Wally. "And, anyway, he's not going anywhere. Wait a bit, until he's better."

"The bugger mightn't get any better," said Trumble, kicking out at some imaginary obstacle.

"Well, all the more reason to let him rest," said Wally. "He's so sick with fever that he could blurt out anything. Who can believe a man so sick?"

"I must have something conclusive for the log." Trumble's worried frown persisted.

"The ramblings of a man in delirium might sully the log, not enhance it," said Tosh, his legalistic turn of phrase helping Wally's argument and giving Trumble pause.

As first mate, Tosh was responsible for making the official log entries from the slate—the course, the distance sailed, wind and prevailing weather and any significant incidents involving the captain and the crew.

"All right. All right. But the moment he's well enough for interrogation, you let me know," he said to Wally. He waddled over to his bunk and gave a sharp wave of dismissal.

Leaving the captain's cabin, Wally made directly for Charlie's little bolt-hole up on the mid-deck.

The black man's condition didn't look good. His tongue was bright red and black vomit stained his bed-shirt. In a weak, scratchy voice he complained of a headache and sore muscles.

"I'm dreaming while I'm awake," he said. "Funny things, like my sister sitting on the stanchion over there. She won't look at me, though. It's a dream isn't it, Doc? She can't be here. She's dead already."

"The fever, Charlie, it's the fever."

"Am I nearly home?"

"Yes, not far now," said Wally.

"You wouldn't tell a man a lie, would you?"

"No, Charlie, of course I wouldn't."

"Thank you, man."

Charlie Spencer died that evening. He was tipped overboard along with all two dozen shiny Martini-Henry rifles. He'd died of the stranger's disease yet he was barely a mile to the south-east of old Port Royal, for centuries the gateway to his Jamaican homeland.

Trumble, for once, looked happy.

25 Good Luck, at Last

With Charlie's passing, a wave of good fortune washed over the *Arabella*, as if the dead Jamaican was rearranging their destiny from heaven. Some of the men even said as much. A heavy load of beef and oranges materialized out of nowhere, though the good graces of the Quarantine Officer couldn't be excluded, and even more heartening, a telegram from the ship's agent instructed Captain Trumble to make for Charleston. Two men with mild fevers bounced back to full health, as if by magic, and no more were struck down. This last miracle Wally ascribed to the muslin mosquito nets, but Tosh was the only one to concur—the others offered their thanks to Charlie.

Wally and Tosh's dinner next night in the captain's cabin had a festive air, with sherry served before the roast beef and port poured after. Spicy ginger biscuits replaced the usual tasteless hard tack and, to cap it all, a somewhat tiddly Mister Blodgett offered each of them a large slice of fruit cake, never mind that it had no icing—cake of any kind was a rarity at sea, kept aside for special occasions: reprieve from a storm, crossing the equator, matters of that sort.

"Charlie has found us a reprieve and we take leave of this hell-hole in the morning," said the captain, rocking back on his chair, his hands resting over his paunch, a picture of full-bellied contentment.

"What a saint," said Tosh and he blew a big puff of cigar smoke in a heavenly direction. Charlie's elevation from untrustworthy bugger to the ranks of the blessed had taken less than forty-eight hours.

The captain nodded in agreement. "We'll make straight for Charleston. With any luck we'll be clear any serious fever and we can make port there—and sell our cargo."

Wally would have liked to have seen Havana, but in the few days it would take to be offshore Cuba's capital, the *Arabella* would still be considered infectious and the crew wouldn't be allowed ashore. It was August now and some said Havana was worse than hell in mid-summer, what with high humidity and a burning sun, yet there'd be ice, music and pretty girls, things a young man trapped on a cramped wooden ship begins to yearn for.

Trumble seemed to read Wally's mind. "And you'll love Charleston, Wally. I know you will. You've not been there before, eh?"

"Yes sir, I'm sure I will."

Wally knew very little about Charleston, other than how it had been a major port for slave trading and how it had been devastated by the Civil War.

"There are people there as rich as any London toff and some of their mansions rival Blenheim Palace, what with their big chandeliers and fancy frescoes, let alone their fountains and flower gardens full of azaleas and rose bushes."

"But without the aristocracy, I assume," said Wally, mindful of the New World's sense of republicanism.

"Maybe not called Your Highness or Your Lordship, but aristocrats in every other sense. Last visit I met a Mister Wade Hampton at the Planters Hotel. Now he's certainly more powerful than any of your English High Muckety-Mucks. He's been Governor of the State of South Carolina and he's got money comin' out his ears, he has. Made it out of cotton and rice and selling indigo back to the old country—they use it to color cloth. A real gentleman, too, and free with his favors."

Trumble wasn't alone in preferring the success of the self-made man; Wally agreed with him in spirit although he certainly wouldn't decline riches if they were encumbered with a fancy title, unlikely as it was that he'd ever be in that position, brown skin and all.

All this talk of grandeur and destiny among the rich and privileged did little to assuage Trumble's irritation next morning when men from a lighter, bringing supplies, passed on the news that the Prince Imperial of France, Louis Bonaparte, had been killed in a skirmish in the Zulu War. Exiled in England, he had joined action with British forces in Africa as an observer but he'd been ambushed while out on patrol.

"Damnable blacks, savages all," he shouted—to the whole world but to no one in particular. Charlie's beatification had been revoked even before the anchor was weighed and Wally's fanciful dream of a peerage spluttered out.

The *Arabella* set sail to the east and north, old Bumble planning to work the ship through the Windward Passage that separates Haiti from the eastern tip of Cuba. This was a shorter route but it entailed a few days of hard sailing, tacking back and forth against strong easterly winds and warm beating rain. The sea cut up a mighty chop and, under reduced sail, the ship creaked and groaned over foamy crests only to slam down heavily into short troughs of grey turbulence.

A few of the men were seasick but none more so than a Chinaman with the incongruous name of Hadji. This man was almost as short as Tosh but in every other respect he was his opposite. He sickened easily and had a fear of climbing the rigging; his way with the English language was as weak as Tosh's was strong.

"Hadji tummy no good," he moaned to Wally. "Hadji stay bunk."

He would be of little use above-decks, Wally reported to Trumble, and in his condition he might well be washed overboard, so weak he was and dispirited, scarcely able to take more than a sip of the beef tea and brandy that Wally offered him.

The captain agreed, on condition that he be transferred to Wally's cabin, so as not to upset the other men with all his retching and groaning.

"And where should I sleep, sir?" asked Wally.

"You can take the Chinaman's hammock. It's just for a few days, isn't it? Anyways you might be needed on deck and in the foc's'le you'll better hear the call."

Neither a hammock nor a call on deck appealed to Wally but Trumble was the captain and Wally was at sea. It wouldn't be the first disappointment he'd suffered on this trip. Losing Charlie Spencer and Reverend Mudd bothered him but somehow the confinement of his little dog, Skipper, troubled him most, not only for the senseless unreasonableness for his banishment but also because the little dog hadn't been able to weigh the risks of following Wally aboard back in Tenerife. Spencer and Mudd had taken their chances—they were grown men and knew things might go bad for them but little Skipper had naively trusted his new master. Wally hadn't been responsible for anyone other than himself before and he felt he'd made a mess he'd made of it.

Aggravated by nausea and pitching about in a hammock, he began to wish he hadn't joined the *Arabella* at all. The Caribbean Sea can look mighty appealing in a vision dreamed in a cold, drafty room in central Glasgow, with wet socks and a stuffed-up nose, but the reality of tropical waters could be a damn sight more frightening, even terrifying, than anything the Clyde could throw at you.

As they approached the Passage off Port-au-Prince, the wind and current turned more favorable. Hadji recovered to his usual state of mild hypochondria and Wally returned to his own cabin. Had there been another outbreak of fever aboard, things might have been very difficult but the ship's new-found good fortune persisted and the net effect of sailing to weather troubled the men little, if at all.

Wally resolved to write a careful account of his experiment with the muslin. Long swathes of it hung lengthwise from hooks above each hammock in the foc's'le and in each cabin. Trumble himself permitted a canopy of sorts to be constructed above his cot, urged to do so by Wally who suggested it would set a proper example for the men.

A true man of science might have arranged things so that some men were kept in the open air, their skin exposed to any mosquito menace. The great nautical experimenter of scurvy fame, James Lind, might have looked kindly on such a plan but Wally was a man of medicine now and he couldn't bear the thought of losing another life in the name of science. He'd be happy enough to see the end of yellow fever aboard the *Arabella* and send copies of his log to Patrick Manson and Arthur Doyle. Maybe Arthur could use the information in another of his stories, so many of them based on facts that others hadn't yet the sense to see.

The sea changed to a bright blue color somewhere off the north of Cuba as they entered the Gulf Stream in the Straits of Florida. They passed to west of Andros Island and Grand Bahama, avoiding the treacherous shallows that bedeviled all the outer islands of the Bahamas chain. These were waters under American control, heavily blockaded by the Union navy during the Civil War, and now criss-crossed by smugglers with cargoes of fiery rum and cheap black labor.

It was, therefore, of no surprise to Trumble that they were intercepted by a revenue cutter.

"Spring-a-luff," he barked to the helmsman, turning the *Arabella* into the wind as the steamship rapidly closed on them, its gleaming swiveling cannon pointing at them and blue-uniformed men at the ready. Black smoke gushed out from its tall funnel and every one of its schooner-rigged sails was tense—a warrior ready to pounce.

The excitement drew almost every man on deck, including Wally who'd never seen a revenue cutter before, but had heard stories of the sometimes bullying tactics used by the revenue men to uncover hidden caches of smuggled goods. Not only might the Arabella's men be roughed up but the boat could be crippled by the chopping away of beams and planks that, to the eye of a revenue officer, might be hiding contraband.

"Should we run up the yellow jack, sir?" called Wally.

"Damned good idea," said Trumble. "We can play our own game, too."

The cutter visibly slowed at the sight of the dreaded pennant and a covey of revenue men, most of them ratings in blue sack coats but a couple officers, capped and wearing epaulettes, gathered in agitated conversation. The standoff lasted no more than a couple of minutes but during that time the *Arabella* was as hushed as a courtroom before the announcement of the verdict, Trumble and his men as tense as any defendant. Then, with a long toot of her whistle and puffing a cloud of black smoke, the revenue cutter abruptly steamed off at a tangent, no doubt unable to hear the derisive, yet relieved, cheers from the ship it left in its wake.

"Great idea, doc," said the captain and he clapped Wally on the back. "From now on I'm going to call you Doctor Yellow Jack."

Watching the cutter as it faded into the distance, Wally noticed things he'd not ever seen before: fish flying across the surface of the water, big brown birds soaring high then diving headfirst into the sea, dolphins as big as any he'd seen off the coast of Otago and then the occasional coconut bobbing in the swells.

"Cor blimey, it's like a zoo, ain't it," said carpenter Edwards, leaning his elbows on the rail beside Wally.

"I never think to look at the water. I'm usually looking at the sky instead," said Wally.

"So you missed the sharks?"

"Here?"

"An hour ago, maybe less. They was polishin' off a dolphin. Big buggers. Three or four of 'em—hard to tell how many with all the thrashin' about and blood curdlin' the water."

"Not a place to swim, then?"

"Last a few minutes, I'd say."

Wally shivered. How was it that some people called the ocean friendly. It wasn't. Hostile, vicious, deadly—they would be better words. When he'd first sailed out of New Zealand he'd been most concerned about drowning, the sea being deep and unforgiving, but there were many more ways to die out here—any one of a myriad of fevers, being set upon by a frenzied crewman, eaten alive by sharks. Compared to these, drowning seemed a rather comfortable way to go, if going it had to be.

Little did Wally know, then, that he would soon have a chance to test these options for himself. Mother Nature was about to turn a deaf ear to Charlie Spencer.

26 The Hurricane

10 October. Day 54. Noon. 26.83N, 79.39W. Wind SE, strong. Bearing 335.

The first day north of Grand Bahama started out quietly enough. Doctor Yellow Jack sat on his bunk and penned a letter to his friend, Arthur Conan Doyle. In bold India ink, he itemized what he'd learned about yellow fever, tidbits to tempt Arthur's appetite for the exotic and the bizarre. That a devious captain might log a yellow fever case as benign remittent fever, to escape quarantine, seemed the kind of pearl that Arthur could weave into one of his stories.

Imagine the havoc that could be wrought, wrote Wally, *if yellow fever was brought into New Orleans that way, or New York City for that matter. Think of the loss of life that would result, a fatal disease running rampant and all due to a single, simple lie, a white lie some might even call it.*

He heard familiar footsteps and turned to see Tosh peering in at him.

"Might be in for a bit of a breeze, Doc," said the first mate, a tight smile on his little face.

"How big's a bit?" Wally asked.

"Come up top. You'll get the idea."

Black clouds crowded the vast sky to the east and the distant sea had turned gray. Lightening flashes lit up the horizon like fireworks, a signal, according to Tosh, that Nature's game with them was about to begin.

Trumble frowned and paced around the afterdeck. "Can we outrun the bugger? Or should we hunker down with a drogue?" He was talking out loud and not expecting an answer, the way muddle-heads do, unable to assess the risks in any rational way. If he'd taken a vote amongst his crew, most would have urged him to go bare-poles, with maybe a storm jib, and ride the storm out that way. After all, this was hurricane season in this part of the world and with Florida to leeward, where could a ship run? But old Bumble never sought their advice.

"Full sail!" he finally called to Tosh. And looking back at the gathering clouds, he added, "Be sharp about it."

Set on a north-west course, the *Arabella* gallantly raced ahead of the advancing storm and for three or four hours she looked a possible winner. The winds were gusting to sixty knots and although the old ship shuddered and sighed, she put on a brave face and ploughed through the growing white-capped swells. The men skidded around the sea-sprayed decks, lightening sail as needed to keep the ship from pitching stern over bow.

But, as the hours rolled on towards night, the wind shrieked ever louder and black walls of water churned over the decks, shaking and stretching the *Arabella*'s every futtock, joint and seam. Wally didn't have to be a seaman to understand the precariousness of the situation. Eighty knots of wind, a hundred, maybe more, the number didn't matter; it was more a question of what would break first. What part of the ship, what rotting spa, what ancient fitting, would be the first to surrender to the feverous pounding of the ocean?

Wally hunkered below with the men in the foc's'le, all hatches battened down, the wind howling outside. Nobody had much to say although a few lips were moving, talking, probably pleading, with their God.

Above the roar of the gale an even more tremendous boom sounded, like an exploding cannon, and the ship heeled sharply to port, not righting herself but instead settling into a lopsided arc of to-and-fro motion, like an gasping elephant brought low by a shot through the shoulder. The lantern light went out and men grabbed blindly for handholds amidst a chaos of tumbling boots, bags and belongings.

"Knockdown! Knockdown!" yelled a strained voice in the dark.

"Oh, my God!" cried another.

Wally wedged himself between two lockers. His heart was racing and he could already feel sweat trickling down his back. He tried to keep calm and recall what Tosh had told him about what would happen if a mast snapped. It wouldn't be pretty, that he knew, but a good crew could apparently take their time, cut the shrouds and pitch the broken mast overboard. Loss of a mast, even the mainmast, wasn't a disaster in and of itself—they could get by with just the mizzen if they had to. But masts don't snap in mild weather, he thought. And just how good will the crew of the *Arabella* be in the midst of a hurricane? The drag of fallen timbers and sails could surely pull the ship under in minutes. If I go up on deck, I'm just asking to be swept overboard. But, if I do nothing, am I not inviting the grim reaper to do his worst.

One of the Tartars lit a lantern and the men clambered their way towards the companionway, ready to swarm out upon the deck. Wally knew that Tosh would be out there already. He knew he had to go above and try to help, no matter that he didn't know how. All hands turn out for a foundering vessel.

The little lascar, Verraswamy, cried out, "Vishnu preserve us!"

"Oh to be in England," echoed the carpenter.

Wally scanned the anxious faces half-lit by the flickering lantern, each depending on his mates and never more in unison. They all, even the youngest of them, an Irish lad no more than fifteen years old, shared a grim smirk as if sealing a covenant, a bond of fellowship, as they were about to embrace the ferocious elements.

"Out we go—and cheerly!" called a voice and the men pushed and shoved their way up onto the deck, the leaders faltering as torrents of sea water pressed at them from above. A deluge of foaming ocean poured through the open hatch but one by one they made it through.

The leaning topside was a confused struggle, with men unable to see one another clearly let alone hear any orders. Instinct told them to grab a line, any line, and fasten themselves tight to the pitching and rolling ship so that rogue waves wouldn't wash them away. The crazy angle of the deck, some of it already submerged, made movement almost impossible and a foothold was anything protruding, a stanchion, a spindle, a block. The starboard life-lines were beyond reach.

Wally grabbed the loose end of a line and yanked it tight around his waist, making a crude knot, and he yanked hard to test it would hold him. He worked his way aft, crab-like, across the slippery, sloping deck to where he could hear the heavy blows of hatchets rising over the roar of the elements.

He could see Tosh, Edwards and a couple of others chopping wildly at the shrouds holding the mast. In between sheets of rain, he spotted the clean break where the thick mainmast had snapped and the shrouds that were the only tethers keeping the mast from toppling into the sea. How like an amputation of a limb, this was, he thought. The mast, once vital but now a useless and life-threatening appendage, must be hacked free of the ship, a sacrifice to a greater good. A ship's surgeon, in battle, must meet a similar challenge: with flak and fire around him he makes his hasty cuts. The enemy here is a hurricane: the wind and waves its weapons.

The mast shuddered and shifted as fewer and fewer constraints held it in place at the edge of the deck. A heavy wobble and a creaking groan accompanied the sounds of tearing sails and snapping sheets and lanyards and the mighty mast rose up, like a sounding whale, and flung itself into the sea.

In the maelstrom of confusion that followed, Wally was dragged flailing overboard, his safety line unfortunately attached not to the ship but to the dismembered mast now bobbing crazily in the waves. The shock of hitting the water, his inability to catch his breath and the dragging pull of the line around his waist kept every other thought from his mind. His situation was so precarious that an awareness of it might well frighten him to death before he had time to drown.

He swung his arms about frantically and he fought to catch some air. Loose lines thrashed around him and, like slippery kelp that could trap a swimmer on a rocky coast, they threatened to drag him under. As he fought to free himself from these menacing tentacles, he careened up against the big mast, the one thing that might just save him. He grabbed onto it for dear life and leveraged himself up for a gulp of air. One big gulp and then another; how sweet they were.

The log bucked wildly like an angry colt and Wally struggled to lash himself more tightly to it. Luckily the spars and sails kept the log from rolling much but he could lose this one chance of salvation in a second if he allowed a wave to wash him off his shabby raft.

His struggle to secure himself on the pitching mast lasted half an hour or more and during that time the intensity of the wind and waves subsided and the rain eased enough to let him look about for any sign of the *Arabella*. The narrow grey horizon was featureless—no ship, no land, just the dark churning waves and misty spume of a postictal ocean.

Every muscle in Wally's body ached and his legs were scratched raw from riding the splintered mast, his injuries compounded because somewhere in the wild wrestlings he had lost his pants. His torso was bound in the manacle of constraints that he had wound around himself; his destination and that of the mast were now the same. But a mast had no life and didn't need to breathe. It could float for weeks, at the mercy of fickle currents and tides, needing neither food nor fresh water. Had he saved himself from drowning only to die a more painful way from thirst and hunger strapped to a wooden cross in a shark-infested sea?

Despondent and fatigued, Doctor Yellow Jack slipped into a groggy sleep.

27 Ashore

How long he slept, he didn't know, but when he awoke he could hear a shrieking sound interrupt the dull whooshing of the waves. It took him a moment to remember where he was, or at least for him to recall that he was lost at sea. The shrieking came from sea-gulls as they wheeled and dove down onto the water to pluck up little silver fish. Wally saw a fin and was at first afraid, but it turned out to belong to a dolphin.

Turning towards the whooshing sound, he spotted a beach just over the waves breaking on the shore. What a welcome sight. Rough brush bordered the beach and a few straggly trees but he could see no sign of habitation.

He struggled to free himself from his bindings, finding the effort most difficult and almost beyond him. Whether it was from fatigue, hunger, thirst or all three, he didn't care; these problems would soon be behind him. As the last cord was loosened he managed to give a little shout, "Hooray! I bloody well made it."

The waves pushed him ashore, rolling him in onto the warm, welcome sand and he lay there exhausted but relieved. His mouth felt like salted leather, his whole body was soggy from long immersion and he was clad only in his old calico tunic, yet he might have been in a tuxedo at a festive dinner so content was he to be on *terra firma*.

Slowly he sat up and surveyed the beach. To the south he could make out a low headland or perhaps the mouth of a river; to the north, there was nothing but beach. The sea was quiet now. No ships were to be seen, the gulls still circled and the sun burned down on him from a cloudless sky. After plucking out several wood splinters from his chafed thighs, he helped himself to his feet and with uncertain steps worked his way south towards the headland.

A river, or perhaps it was a lagoon, emptied into the sea beyond the headland and Wally's hope of finding someone settled on his heading inland along the edge of the tidal estuary. The sand was firmer here and he spotted crabs and lizards near the high water mark. If he had to, he could always eat such things. A Maori lives off the land, he reminded himself, and he scanned the brush for edible plants but all he saw were tough fibers of sun-dried grasses and woody bushes like the gnarled manuka of his home-land.

"Hey, boy! Whatcha up ta?" The loud voice startled Wally and he swung around with his fists up.

A big, pointy-faced man in torn, blue breeches stood on the bank above him, reaching towards him with the tip of a fishing pole as if about to prod an uncooperative cow.

"Where's your pants?" the big man said, using the rod as a pointer as if Wally might've been unaware of his deficiency.

"Excuse me, sir," said Wally, "but I fell off my ship. I got nothin'."

"Well you better get somethin' soon because the Carlton boys will whip your colored ass if they see you like that." He gave a coarse snort and started to limp away.

"No, please, could you help me," begged Wally. "I can't go much further."

"Help? You sound like *ma femme*."

"I'll pay you," said Wally. "I'll make it worth your while." It was a lie, of course, but Wally was desperate.

"And your money's where? In your pants, I bet."

"I can get some, don't worry. I'm a doctor."

Later, Wally would learn that it was this medical boast, not the offer of money that turned the big man with blue breeches in his favor, but for now, he was simply pleased to be making headway.

The big man was a fisherman, an Acadian calling himself Possum LeBlanc, and his hut stood a mere hundred yards back from the estuary. Built of driftwood and with a thatched roof, the low one-room shack was an untidy mess of empty whiskey bottles, coconuts and life's bare essentials: a blanket, a tin plate, a fork and wash basin, or more correctly, a big turtle shell that doubled as a water receptacle. A couple of fishing poles rested against one wall and tangled bits of line adorned the others. Various size hooks, a pencil and a few scraps of white note-paper were scattered on top of a crate which served as Possum's dining table, work bench and writing desk. The smell of dead fish and stale liquor curdled the dank Florida air.

The big man dug around and found an old pair of pants for Wally and a hat made of straw. He reached into his food safe and with a fishing knife he carved off a chunk of dried beef for Wally to chew along with the tea he'd boiled up. A mug of whiskey seemed to be all he needed for himself and he downed it in one long gulp.

"A doctor, you say? Well, what do you think of this?" Possum lifted a leg of his pants to reveal a jagged wound above his right ankle. The raised and angry edges gaped and oozed green pus and red streaks traveled up the leg as far as Wally could see.

"This needs to be cleaned," said Wally. "And bandaged properly."

"I wash it in the sea each morning."

"A shark do it?"

"More?" said Possum, pointing at what remained of the dried beef. He sliced off another lump and tossed it onto the tin plate. The wizened-up old meat clattered like a stone, but Wally did not refuse it. "A gator. He's a dead gator now. And I sprinkle capsicum on it—to bring the blood to the surface, you know." He pointed to a big jar of red pepper which was sitting beside the crate.

"I'll need to scrape it first and then we can cover it with strips of cloth what've been boiled."

Possum slugged back another mug of whiskey. "I'm ready," he said.

"Tomorrow. First thing tomorrow," said Wally. "I've got to sleep now. I'm so tired I couldn't scratch my nose."

But the whiskey had loosened Possum's tongue and he rambled on about all the fish he caught for Dan Carlton and his family and how they repaid him with food and liquor. He talked about his last five years on the estuary and how he'd seen new settlers come and go, some back home and others to their grave. He spoke about the mosquitoes, the panthers and the snakes, the Seminoles and the Cubans, and how many cows the Carltons had. He explained to Wally that the nearest settlement was Fort Pierce, on the other side of the lagoon, and that he paddled his little boat over there every now and again, to mail a letter or read a newspaper.

But Wally never heard him say these things because he was sound asleep.

28   *The New Arrival*

The next few days were taken up with cleaning and dressing the fisherman's leg wound, a challenge under any circumstance but especially difficult when the scalpel was a fishing knife and the bandages were strips of an old cotton shirt. However, the final result looked much healthier and Wally declared that Possum wouldn't lose his leg.

Wally's own strength returned and he walked back down the beach to where he had been washed up. The mast, his life-raft of sorts, lay deeply anchored in sand above the water line. Wally cut free some shreds of sail and rigging still clinging to the spars and prepared to haul them back to the fisherman's camp. They might be of use as bedding or perhaps insulation for the walls of the hut which streamed with water during every thunderstorm.

When he pulled his load higher up the beach to where the sand was firmer and the going easier, a scrap of twilled black fabric caught his eye, half buried in sand. Wally used his hands to dig out the cloth which proved to be a sailor's jacket, not identifiable to him but very possibly off the *Arabella*.

These last few days, he hadn't dared to think about the fate of his ship and his friends. Had his shipmates survived the storm or were they now deep in Davy Jones's locker? Might his being washed off the deck been his salvation, a miracle of good fortune, a gift from Charlie to the doctor who tried to ease his fevered agonies? And what of Skipper?

The fisherman welcomed the scraps of sail and line and he cast them up onto a hoard of flotsam he'd stashed behind his shack. His limp was less noticeable now and he hummed a little tune while he sat at his crate-table gutting and filleting small fish in the light of a kerosene lamp.

"Fancy we go visit the town?" he said, with a toothy grin.

"Tomorrow?" said Wally.

"I'll show you the sights," said Possum. "Not there's much to see."

Wally might be able to get his hands on a newspaper. Maybe there'd be news of the *Arabella*.

"And I can show off my doctor," said Possum, raising his pointy nose with his forefinger, in a mock aristocratic way.

"Like a freak show?" said Wally.

"Yeah, and I'll collect the *honoraires*—the fees."

The next morning's windy chop buffeted Possum's dinghy but the big fisherman scarcely seemed to notice. He sang a song, in French or maybe Creole, and boasted to Wally about his days growing up in Terrebonne parish, Louisiana and how he wished he still had his accordion. But, of course, all that was behind him now, abandoned in haste as he made his escape from villains unknown, at least unknown to Wally, and he thought it better not to enquire too deeply. Who knows what Possum had really been up to?

That the British had been rough on the Acadians in Canada and that most had been exiled back to France or down to Louisiana was about all that Wally knew of their culture, a downtrodden splinter of society with odd language habits and a closeness with poverty. People like that in London were attracted to crime like moths to a candle, and why should Possum be any different?

They made their way through a heavy downpour to Captain Hogg's store, the center of gossip in the little town and the most likely place to hear news of a shipwreck. A man behind a simple counter was transacting business with a couple of native Indians—*Seminoles* said Possum—who wanted jars of brandied cherries and peaches in exchange for deer hides. After much haggling back and forth a deal was struck which seemed to satisfy both parties.

Wally surveyed the well-stocked shelves. He spotted saws and machetes, axes and hoes, harnesses and saddles, packaged groceries and cans of food, a mix of candies and a shelf of patent medicines. Sacks of flour and sugar lay limp against the wall but barrels of tea and coffee beckoned with a lively mix of pleasing aromas.

"Benjamin Hogg," the storekeeper said, reaching out to shake Wally's hand. "I don't know if I like your company," he added, giving a wink and nodding in Possum's direction.

"Wally McConnochie."

"*Doctor* McConnochie," said Possum. He had something more precious than deer hides on offer.

"And a hint of Scotland, do I gather?" Hogg looked at Wally with the cool eye of experienced appraiser.

"Yes, sir," said Wally. "My dad is—was—Scottish and I took my degree in Glasgow. But I'm really from New Zealand."

"You'll have to meet my Annie then," said Hogg.

"Annie?"

"My bonnie wife. She hails from Glasgow and she doesn't meet many of her kinfolk down here."

Plans were made for Possum and Wally to come back to the store at six o'clock that evening.

The Hoggs lived above the shop and Benjamin promised the both of them a fine meal as guests. How could they refuse? No time had been spent on why Wally was in town, no discussion of his shipwreck and no questions asked about the *Arabella*. Would that all come later?

Wally looked most un-doctor-like that evening as Benjamin Hogg ushered him up the stairs to meet his wife. His tunic was in tatters and his borrowed pants were held up by a length of twine. His feet were bare and, in his hand, he carried the straw hat loaned to him by Possum. He also hadn't shaved for the best part of a week.

"Pleased to meet you, ma'am," he said, tentatively offering his somewhat grubby hand.

Annie Hogg was a smart-looking woman in her mid-thirties, her dark hair pulled back in a bun and her eyes full of smiles. In Glasgow she might have been the wife of a doctor or a clergyman, someone accustomed to entertaining and to offering comfort to the needy.

"You're new here, Doctor, I take it."

"I was washed overboard in big storm, three days ago, or was it four."

"Och, washed in by the hurricane tide, were you? I might well believe it." She honed in on Wally's predicament in an instant, intelligence and intuition unmasking him despite his ridiculous attire. "You were lucky to survive. We had a grim enough time here on so-called dry land."

She turned to her husband. "Ben, show the good doctor to the bathroom so he can wash up and shave. And bring him up a set of clothes from the store, something fitting for a man of learning. Socks and boots, too, while you're at it."

Wally's half-hearted objections were not accepted and Benjamin Hogg led him off to the bathroom, along with a bucket of warm water and a scrubbing brush.

"My razor's over here," said Hogg, pointing to a metal basin, "and here's a towel to use." Not for a long time had Wally felt so much at home. Indeed he hadn't often felt as much at home even when he was.

An hour later, washed, shaved and smartly clothed, he re-appeared in the Hogg's parlor.

"Feel better?" said Annie Hogg.

"I scarcely know myself," said Wally, catching a glimpse of himself in a big mirror. "I must thank you very much and, of course, I will repay you—"

"Oh, shut your trap," she said. "Nothing we would'na do for any Scot, a wee bitty down on their luck."

"And now a toast," said Benjamin, handing a glass of golden-brown liquid to Possum and Wally. "To your good health," he added, raising his own glass.

"Oh, excuse me," said Annie, "I mustn't forget the turkey." She hurried out of the room towards the kitchen.

Heavy rain rattled the tin roof and cabbage palms clattered in the wind as Wally lounged back sipping the finest Scotch whisky he'd ever tasted. The evening had just begun.

29 A Chilling Telegram

When Annie and Benjamin offered Wally a couple of rooms at the back of the store, he accepted without hesitation. There was only one condition and that was that he work as a doctor in the little town, lancing boils, pulling teeth and setting fractures, the kind of things country doctors did everywhere. He would be paid next to nothing but his room and food would be free and Benjamin would make sure that he never lacked for a warm set of clothes and a good pair of boots.

Wally's work brought him face to face with sun-shriveled cowboys, salt-caked fisherman and dark-skinned Indians. He patted the heads of black babies, tipped his hat to uniformed militiamen and learned a few words of Seminole. He tasted grits, corn and alligator, peanuts, rice and frog legs, all manner of foods foreign to him but staples in Florida. At night, beyond the buzz of circling mosquitoes, he'd hear giant toads sing in croaky chorus, armadillos sniffing and snorting and raccoons rummaging through the garbage pit. The insane shrieks of limpkins would sometimes trigger nightmares. Egrets, pelicans and eagles he'd seen before but never in such numbers. I've landed in a tropical zoo, he thought, so different from New Zealand where the animal kingdom is mostly sheep, cattle and rabbits.

Not all the animals in the zoo were friendly, however. One old drover veered away from Wally whenever he saw him in the street. Another spat on the ground each time they passed.

"Is it my color?" he asked Benjamin.

"No," said the older man. "It's not that. White, black, brown is all the same to us down here. Course, if you was up north ..."

"Well, what the hell is it?"

"There's been talk." Benjamin shifted his weight from one foot to the other as if he had ants in his boots.

"About what? What kind of talk?"

Benjamin lowered his voice to a whisper. "About you being some kind of Jonah. Maybe you're responsible for all the wet weather we been having."

"What rubbish," said Wally, waving his arms in exasperation. "Where do they get that stupid idea from?"

"The story of how you came here—falling off a ship in a storm. Maybe you were thrown overboard, like Jonah, to save the ship."

"And I suppose I was swallowed by a whale," said Wally, with a scoffing laugh. Wally's father had been a whaler and he often told Wally the biblical story of Jonah and the whale, as much a powerful piece of sailor mythology as religious parable.

"You asked me what others were saying. Mind you, I don't agree with them. They're just simple folk and a touch suspicious."

That night, and for the next few nights, Wally mulled over his options, tossing and turning in the humid darkness. He could simply ignore the gossipers, superstitious nitwits that they were, or he could tackle them head on, confront them with the stupidity of their accusations and settle things with his fists, if needed. He could also move on, head north, and maybe catch a ship back to London or Liverpool.

But where would that get me, he thought? I wasn't comfortable there before. Why would I be more comfortable there now?

He pictured the crowded and dirty streets of London, the cold, dark alleys where assassins lurked, the brutish, drunk, beer-swillers and the screeching molls they dragged behind them, the world of Mudlips and Kembles.

Yet that was the only London he knew, that and the inside of a pub or a working-mans' hostel. How could he ever hope to fit into the more decorous society of doctors and lawyers, he now a full-fledged practitioner of medicine himself?

New Zealand had limited appeal to him, as well. Wouldn't I feel like a child again if I slunk back to Kirimoko and Kotuku, he thought? Have I come all this way for naught? I owe it to myself to make a go of it here, in a place where I have much respect and even better prospects.

And what of his friends on the *Arabella*? Were they safe? Did they survive the storm—Tosh, Trumble and Samuel Edwards? Skipper? Or was he the only one to escape the storm? The arguments went round and round and Wally worked himself into deeper and deeper despondency.

Annie Hogg must have seen that something was unsettling him because one morning at breakfast she asked, "Are you sleeping all right, Wally? You look so drawn these days."

"Oh, I'm fine, very fine," he said. "But I do worry some about my friends."

"On your ship? Of course, you must be worried." She wrung her hands on her apron. "We can send off a telegram or two to chase them down. They're bound to be holed up somewhere celebrating their own good luck and offering toasts to your fond memory. Where was it you say the *Arabella* was headed?"

All communication with the outside world was funneled through the postmaster, a fussy little man with big round spectacles and a leather eyeshade. He ran the telegraph machine and dispatched the mail from an office, simply a desk and chair enclosed in a ramshackle hut. However unassuming the premises, they were the nerve center of Fort Pierce.

"Two pictures of Ol' Rough'n'Ready and a telegram," he said. "That'll be twenty cents."

Wally handed over a couple of dimes. The five cent stamps he would use to mail off letters to his mother and to Arthur. "How long before I get a reply to the telegram, you think?"

"Stop by tomorrow, around noon. They're usually pretty prompt. The harbormaster, I mean."

Wally's cabled message was simple—has the *Arabella* shown up in Charleston? Two weeks had passed since the storm, plenty of time for a crippled ship to reach the port or to send a message they were safe and sound.

The reply, next day, however, was ominous. NO CONTACT FROM ARABELLA STOP LONDON PERPLEXED STOP LLOYDS NOTIFIED STOP MILTON BAGWELL HARBORMASTER CHARLESTON

The reference to Lloyds, the big maritime insurer, sent a chill through Wally. To him it meant that the shipping agent in London was assuming the worst—the *Arabella* was lost. Fine Jonah I turned out to be, he thought.

All thought of his shipmates was put on hold when fists pounded on Wally's door late that night.

What on earth can this be, he thought? Who's after me now? And for what? He lit a candle and stumbled towards the door.

"I'm coming," he called, as the fists banged again on. "Who is it?"

Dan Carlton Jr., son of the biggest cattle baron in Brevard County, stood on the doorstep, wide-eyed and soaking wet, gripping the reins of his panting horse. A cloud of mosquitoes danced around his head.

"My dad—he's dying. Come quick."

"Settle down, Junior! What's the problem?"

"He's got a belly pain so bad he's a screamin' to be put out of his misery."

"Whereabouts in his belly?"

"Down below, near his privates."

"Go fetch me a horse then. Mr. Hogg—he'll help you."

The mercy dash proceeded at a furious pace. Hogg insisted on accompanying them, old man Carlton being his best customer and all. Wally bundled ether and a makeshift surgical kit into a big saddlebag and, wrapped in heavy oilskin capes, they galloped full-speed out onto the trail to the Carlton property. The relentless rain had flooded much of the trail and the rest was little more than a mudslide. At any moment a horse might go down or a man might be thrown.

Yet they made it, mud-splattered and worn, and they crashed through the front door of the homestead, Hogg carrying the saddlebag of medical kit over his shoulder. Any other night, Wally might have smiled at the cattleman's daughters and commented on the finery of their dresses, so unusual such prettiness seemed in this rough man's country, but he was drawn instead to the coarse loud groans coming from the back of the house, more the sound of a wounded bear than of a man, but unmistakably uttered by someone—something—in pain.

Carlton lay naked, sprawled across a large bed, his right hand cradling a large swelling in his right groin and his left hand clutching a near-empty whiskey bottle. His face was contorted with pain and covered in sweat. Someone had made an effort to mop up dark green vomit from off the floor adjacent. The smell in that room was a blend of bar-room and mortuary, life and death.

"Mr. Carlton, I'm the doctor from town," said Wally.

"Bloody hell! Give me something for this pain," replied Carlton, his body twisting in another spasm.

"I want to ask you a few questions first."

"Fix the pain, damn you!"

"I will if you give me just one minute. I have to figure out what's the problem."

Carlton squeezed his eyes closed and puckered his face in a gesture of despairing acceptance.

Wally gently but firmly prized back the cattleman's right hand, revealing a large hernia, distended and ominously reddened. He knew it was too tender to prod.

"How long have you had this swelling, sir?"

"A couple of years."

"And the pain?"

"Four hours—six—no more than that." The man squeezed the words out between gritted teeth.

"Then maybe it's not too late," said Wally, reaching into the saddlebag for the laudanum. "Take a good long swig of this. It'll dull the pain until I put you to sleep."

"You gonna do away with me?" Carlton said it in a way that suggested he might be happy to accept.

"I hope not. But I do need to operate and we must put you to sleep for that."

"Do your damnedest, Doc." The rancher's breathing was irregular and labored and his next words were scarcely audible. "And good luck."

No doubt the old man has seen some gory sights in his cattle work, thought Wally. Let's hope he has enough of his old bull strength left to see him through this.

They carried him through to the kitchen table and covered much of him with a bed-sheet, leaving just his head and his belly exposed. Wally assigned Mrs. Carlton the task of sterilizing his surgical instruments in a pot of water boiling on the stove: a scalpel, forceps, two retractors, a pair of scissors and three needles—a paltry armamentarium but, Wally mused, this battle will be won or lost in a mere ten minutes. A loop of bowel was twisted—strangulated—inside that hernia: if the tissue is still vital when I untwist it, Carlton will live, if not, no surgeon in the world can save him.

Dan Jr. would be his assistant and Ben Hogg his anesthetist. There was little time to show them what they had to do but in five minutes with each of them Wally explained to the younger Carlton how to hold a retractor and to Hogg how to drip ether onto the muslin cloth he laid over the cattleman's nose and mouth, slowly and only on a signal from Wally.

The instruments cooled in the pot, now emptied of water, and Wally nodded to Hogg: time to start dripping. The cattleman was already drowsy from the laudanum—his cries had dissolved into gurgles, half chokes, half snores—and only a few drops of ether were needed to push him through the curtain to unconsciousness.

Wally splashed cold carbolic over the hernia and over his bare hands and he gently spread the skin taut ready for the incision. Old Carlton didn't flinch.

"You can back off the ether now, Ben," said Wally. He looked across the table to Dan Jr. "Ready?"

The younger man nodded but his eyes showed the fear he felt.

The scalpel drew a deep incision across the bulging hernia and Wally quickly cut through the subcutaneous tissue down to the peritoneal sac covering the prolapse.

In less than a minute he could see the strangulated segment of bowel. It looked a dusky blue, almost black, but yet intact. It had not perforated, at least not yet. With Dan Jr. retracting the wound edges, he used forceps and scissors to enlarge the hole in the external and internal oblique muscles through which the bowel had migrated and, very gently, he tried rotating the piece of ileum, because that's what it appeared to be, first one way then the other. With a satisfying flip, it straightened out, and quickly regained a healthier pinkish hue.

"Thank God," said Wally. He looked about him—at Dan Jr., at Ben Hogg and at Mrs. Carlton. "I think he's gonna be alright."

"But he's losing so much blood," said Mrs. Carlton, eyes wide with horror and gnawing on her index finger.

"Oh, that's nothin', Ma," said Dan Jr. "Dad could lose ten times that and not miss a beat. Right, Doc?"

Wally laughed and so did Ben Hogg. The atmosphere lightened like a fresh dawn morning.

"Mop with the towel, young Dan," said Wally, "and I'll close up with some good strong silk. We don't want your dad to have to go through this again."

31 A Future

Old man Carlton recovered his appetite in short order and he celebrated by eating thick slabs of beefsteak washed down with corn whiskey and by smoking long cheroots rolled from black tobacco. As if reprieved from a hanging, he embraced life with new vigor. He ordered the family to join him each evening in prayer and he vowed never more to cuss out his long-suffering wife and children. This blossoming of vitality lifted the spirits of all around him.

He was back on his horse in less than two weeks and his first ride was into town to visit Wally. He barged into Wally's little room at the back of Hogg's shop, muddy boots and overcoat notwithstanding.

"I can never thank you enough," he boomed, shaking Wally's hand so hard he almost broke it.

"I'm pleased you're better," said Wally.

"Better? I've never felt so good—and all because if you." He waved his riding gloves in Wally's face.

"Well ..." Wally felt his face start to flush.

"Don't you be thinking I'm not grateful," Carlton continued.

"No, I don't—."

"Because we've got work to do here."

"Oh, do we? Let me see your stitches." Wally wondered if the old man had sprung a fever. Maybe he'd been on the sauce. Or was it brain damage from the ether?

"No. No. Let me fill you in on a secret first. Sit down, doc, this'll take a while."

Wally sat on the couch he used for patients and motioned the older man to the one chair, the one he himself was using, a wicker high-back loaned to him by Annie Hogg.

Dan Carlton removed his gloves and stuffed them in his now unbuttoned overcoat pocket. He leaned forward in a somewhat conspiratorial manner and belched.

He might have been a coarse old cracker, tough on his cow-hands and unschooled in finer feelings but the dream he shared with Wally was, considering the rustic circumstances of its origins, imaginatively equal to the proudest invention of the celebrated engineer Isambard Kingdom Brunel, builder of Britain's finest ships, bridges and tunnels.

Carlton talked at length and painted a grand future for the little town of Fort Pierce. The land was fertile and the fishing good. Soon the railroad would come and settlers from the north, sick of the cold and crowded condition of their cities would flock in by the thousands.

Carlton planned to incorporate Fort Pierce as a town and run it as a big business venture—a ranch with people, not cows, is what he said, but Wally knew what he meant. There would be work for loggers, carpenters and boat builders, a livery barn and a blacksmith. A church needed building as did a court house, town hall and sheriff's office. Shops in Titusville could open branches down here and teachers would be brought in to set up a school. Of course, the men should have two or three saloons, high class places where they could play cards and have a sing-a-long, but no violence, mind you. Land values would rocket and the town's founders would reap rich profits.

"And that's where you come in," he said, beaming at Wally.

The old man was in full stride and didn't wait for any response from Wally.

"I want you to build a hospital."

Wally smiled a weak smile. He hadn't yet decided to stay in Fort Pierce, a place where some thought he was a Jonah and where he lived as a guest in a back room of a shop, sleeping on a borrowed bed and wearing clothes gifted to him.

"Of course, I'll grant you the land and I'll have my men build it. There's a plot over on Pine St that should be just perfect—good drainage and plenty of shade trees."

"That's a most generous offer, Mr. Carlton, but I'm kinda new here. You don't really know me yet."

172

"I know what I know and that's enough for me," said Carlton, unbuckling his belt to show off his stitches, as if they were proof enough of Wally's competence and good intentions.

"Think about it, lad," he added. "You can build a fine future here."

From that day on, people treated Wally as one of them. Any talk of Jonah or mention of his color evaporated and he was routinely greeted with smiles, handshakes and pats on the back. Never before had he received such attention.

The rains eased and, in bright sunshine, Wally surveyed the nearby swamp lands, making plans for drainage projects that would end the blight of mosquitoes. He put in orders for more tinctures and pills, an umbrella stand, an iron bed, a couple of rugs, assorted pictures and a new jug and basin. He penned a letter to Arthur and asked him to send a copy of Samuel Cooper's Dictionary of Surgery. The younger Carlton and Ben Hogg made him promise that they could assist him in future operations. They had a taste for the grist and gore of surgery and wanted more.

News came through, by telegram, that the *Arabella* was indeed safe. She'd taken a beating after the dismasting but had limped into St Augustine where she was now in refit. The crew were safe, as was his dog, and Captain Trumble exhorted him to join them within the week.

The thought of going back to sea did not appeal to Wally. He'd had enough of Doctor Yellow Jack. And what prospects could he count on in London? Even were he to return to his New Zealand homeland, what chance was there that he would succeed?

He thought of his mother, Kirimoko, and he pictured her singing to him as he nestled in his bed, almost asleep:

E rua tau ruru
E rua tau wehe
E rua tau mutu
E rua tau kai
Two years of wind and storm
Two years when food is scarce
Two years of failing crops, then
Two years of abundant food

The message she implanted in his brain when he was a little boy had meaning now. He had served his time in wind and storm and he had had his fill of fights and fevers. Kirimoko would want him now to have his fill of the good life. This he knew and, with that, he also knew the answer he must send back to the *Arabella*.